TRACK THE MEN DOWN

Also by Lee Martin

Shadow on the Mesa
Fast Ride to Boot Hill
The Last Wild Ride
The Grant Conspiracy: Wake of the Civil War
Fury at Cross Creek
In Mysterious Ways
Revenge at Rawhide
The Maverick Gun
Fury at Sweetwater Pass
The Lone Rider
Black River
Dead Man's Trail
Valley of the Lawless

The Darringer Brothers Series:
Trail of the Fast Gun
Trail of the Long Riders
Trail of the Hunter
Trail of the Circle Star
Trail of the Restless Gun
Trail of the Dangerous Gun

and coming soon…
The Danger Trail

TRACK THE MEN DOWN

LEE MARTIN

VACA MOUNTAIN PRESS
VACAVILLE, CALIFORNIA, USA

Vaca Mountain Press
Paperback ISBN 13: 978-1-952380-41-9
Kindle ISBN 13: 978-1-952380-42-6

Also available in
Large Print ISBN 13: 978-1-952380-43-3

Library of Congress Catalog Card Number: 93-90763

Interior design by Eddie Vincent, ENC Graphic Services
Cover design by Christopher Wait for ENC Graphic Services
Cover images © Getty Images

Published by Vaca Mountain Press

Visit Lee Martin Westerns on Facebook.

To all of my wonderful family,
and in the fond memory of
my beloved mother,
my beautiful sister Arlene,
our rough riding brothers,
and for Jim Liontas.

TRACK THE MEN DOWN

ONE

"**B**last you, Tanner, I ain't tellin' you nothin'."

The wiry man with beady eyes and yellow teeth was sitting alone in a smoky saloon in El Paso, his hands still gripping his poker cards, his companions having hurriedly left the table. He glared up at his accuser.

Will Tanner, black hair cropped to his shoulders, dark eyes fierce, features rough and cheekbones high in a face too weathered for his twenty-eight years, was big and lean and hard of muscle. He was wearing twin Colts and a wide-brimmed black Stetson, a black leather vest over a blue shirt with a red bandanna, and looking all the more like the grim hunter he had become. His voice was heavy with aged fury.

"You was one of 'em, Cory."

"I don't know what you're talkin' about. You're nothin' but a bounty hunter, and I ain't wanted. Now get out of here and leave me alone."

"There was twelve of you. Five are dead. Beeker's dyin' in prison, and he spilled his guts to cut his sentence. One of the name's he gave out was Cory."

"Lots of men named Cory."

Frustrated, Will knew the man was right. Yet his every instinct told him this was the right Cory. He noticed that everyone in the saloon had backed out of the line of fire, but nothing was happening. Cory was too smart to give himself away. But like the other five who had died, Cory would not let it rest.

Will grimaced. "I heard you was tryin' to send a telegram to McBride or Walkersville, up in Colorado territory. Only there ain't no telegraph either place. Is that where I'll find Grissom and the others?"

"I don't know nothin'."

Will turned his back and walked toward the swinging doors where the Texas sunlight was filtering through the smoke. Sweat on his back, he took two steps, listening intently, and then he heard it.

The click of a hammer.

He spun and darted aside, his right six-gun leaping into his palm and firing as Cory's bullet whistled by his left ear. Will's slug hit the wiry man square in the chest.

Cory gasped and jerked, then slumped in his chair, dropping his six-gun to grab at the blood spiraling from him. He stared as Will took hold of the table and threw it aside.

"Here comes that ranger," someone said.

Will holstered his weapon and bent over the wide-eyed Cory. "Where's Grissom?"

Cory gasped and died in his chair. Will straightened, his face burning, angry at himself. If he had taken more time, the man might still be alive, but if he had, Will would be the one lying in his own blood.

The Texas Ranger, a stout man with a square face and

slouch hat, a badge on his cloth vest, came to check the body. Witnesses willingly told him what happened because Cory was nobody's friend.

"It was a fair fight," the bartender added.

At Will's request, the dead man's pockets were searched for letters or addresses, to no avail. The ranger followed Will outside into the sunlight where Will ex-plained who Cory was. The ranger was surprised.

"I thought the Grissom Gang was all dead."

"Buried five of 'em a few years ago. Put Beeker in prison. The others disappeared. But Beeker was dyin' and wanted out, so he gave the only names he could remember. Grissom and Cory. But he didn't live long enough to say what they looked like."

"I'm sure there's a reward out on Cory."

"Hold it for me. I'm headin' north."

The ranger pushed his hat back. "Grissom and his men were Confederate guerillas. And you're a Texan. Must be somethin' personal in this."

"You can count on it."

"But you've hunted others for years."

"Had to have money to live on while I was waitin' for 'em to surface. And I was always hopin' one of the others belonged to Grissom."

"And this has been your whole life?"

"For eight years."

"You can tell me it's none of my business, Mr. Tanner, but is it worth it?"

Will swallowed. "I got no choice."

They shook hands, and Will mounted his black gelding. He headed north, knowing he was but a shadow of the youth who had once laughed and kicked up his heels, a cowhand who had practiced with his six-guns day and night as he hunted the Grissom Gang, practiced until his Army Colts would leap into his hands faster than the eye could see.

It was late spring when he reached Pueblo, where he obtained directions to head for the foothills and follow Little Rocky River west toward the shining, snowcapped mountains. He was told Walkersville was north of the river and McBride was on the south.

Little Rocky River was a busy, rushing stream some three feet deep where it was shallow and twenty feet across, but often narrowing in deep rock chasms. He found the hills to be lush with yellow flowers, dotted with pines and aspens, while cottonwoods and choke-cherry lined the river.

Still a day's ride from the towns, he made camp by a cottonwood along the south side of the stream where it rushed through a deep, narrow gorge in the rocks. His hobbled horse grazed some distance away.

In the early morning, he started breakfast over the small campfire. Nearby in the brush, a small, striped chipmunk was exploring the safety of his presence. Above in the cottonwood, a woodpecker with dotted white breast was making noise.

Abruptly, a thunder of hooves came from the north side of the river. He got to one knee, six-gun in his right hand, waiting and watching. The little chipmunk's tail went straight up, and it darted into the brush. The woodpecker stopped. The singing of the river was overrun by the roar of the hoofbeats.

Then he saw them, two roan horses springing into the air from the north side and sailing across toward his camp. One of the horses kicked over his frying pan as it passed. Both riders reined up some sixty feet away, then came riding back.

Will was furious as he stood up, still holding his Colt.

The riders came closer in the early light. One rider was a young man about eighteen with a lean gangly body, a freckled face flushed with color, laughing blue eyes, and bright red hair that curled under his hat as he pushed it back.

The other rider was a woman in her early twenties with dark red hair thick around her neck and down her back. A lock dangled on her forehead from under her wide-brimmed hat, held down by a chin strap. Despite convention, she was astride in some kind of riding skirt and a man's jacket. She had a right pretty face with freckles and large blue eyes. And she was laughing.

Both had rifles in their scabbards but no other visible weapons. They were so happy and full of life, Will could only gaze at them with envy as he holstered his Colt and tipped his hat to the young woman.

The grinning youth leaned on the pommel of his saddle. "Hey, mister, we're sorry, but she beats me every time, and I was sure lookin' to win."

"You coulda got shot."

"We didn't know anyone was here," she said. "I'm Darcie McBride. This is my brother Ricky."

"Will Tanner."

"Hey, do I smell bacon?" Ricky asked.

"Not anymore. You knocked it over."

Ricky dismounted and came over to the fire. "Well, it ain't cooked yet, and you got another slab there. Let's wipe it off and get on with it. That is if we're invited."

Will nodded but was trying to remain annoyed. Ricky

5

recovered the bacon, wiped it off and threw it back in the pan, then cut another few slices and built up the fire again.

Darcie dismounted and took time to loosen the cinches before removing the bridles and hobbling the horses' front legs so they could nibble at the sweet spring grass. Then she came over where Ricky was busy frying bacon and heating up the beans. She sat across from Will.

"Ricky thinks he's so smart," she said, smiling.

"My sister is too big for her britches."

"Ricky is just a kid."

"My sister is gettin' to be an old lady."

"Ricky hasn't won one race yet."

"Can't figure out why not. She weighs three times as much as me."

She made a face. "That's not so."

Then the two McBrides laughed, and Darcie's freckles danced on her face as she giggled. Will was re-signed to their company and sat down while Ricky served a mighty delicious breakfast. Bacon and beans had never tasted so good.

Ricky poured more coffee. "We ain't never seen you around here before. You goin' to work for Walker?"

"Who?"

"Walker. He owns most everything around here, and he hires a lot of men with guns. And you got two of 'em."

Will shrugged. "I'm not lookin' for work."

"Me, neither," Ricky said, grinning. "We got us a small place in the foothills with a couple hundred head, but me and Darcie, we got to have fun once in a while. We got a kid brother who looks after Mom when we ain't around. Toby's only nine, but he's made it his job."

Will felt his insides bum. Nine years old. His son would have been eight and a few months, riding with him, helping him fix fence, learning to rope and shoot, laughing the way these McBrides were laughing.

Darcie sipped her coffee. "And Mom thinks I should be in the kitchen makin' biscuits. But as long as I can beat Ricky, I'm stayin' in the saddle."

"I can throw a rope better'n you," Ricky said.

"From the saddle maybe, because you got those long arms. But in the corral on foot in a bunch of horses, I'm the one who can throw the hooley-ann. I can make that loop stand on end."

Ricky just grinned as he poured more of the fresh hot coffee, and they sat enjoying the fresh morning air and the song of the river.

"Where are you from, Mr. Tanner?" she asked.

"Texas, mostly."

To Will's surprise, Ricky took out his harmonica.

"We got to pay for our breakfast, Mr. Tanner."

Ricky started his music, hands cupped over the instrument set between his lips, playing lively tunes with a skill and talent that was unexpected. The music filled the air, shutting out the rest of the world. Then Ricky rested, sipping more of his coffee.

"Do you play a musical instrument?" she asked.

Will shrugged. "Guitar. And fiddle."

"So did our father."

"A long time ago," Will added.

Ricky started playing again, and then Darcie began to sing along with him. She had a clear soprano voice, so sweet it sent chills running down Will's back. She sang "Red River Valley," and then skipped to' 'Sweet Betsy from Pike."

As the harmonica played lilting tunes and Darcie sang even as she laughed, Will leaned back on his elbow, watching them and remembering a time when he would have been singing along with them. A time blotted out by the last eight years, until now. These two were dredging up his buried memories, exposing the pain.

"Uh, oh," Ricky said. "Listen. Riders comin'. I bet it's some of Walker's men."

"There's their scout," Darcie said with a laugh, pointing to a turkey buzzard circling overhead.

They sat quiet as four riders approached from the south, all rough looking in ranch clothes except for one wearing conchos on his hatband and gun belt. A gunslinger if there ever was one, his thin mustache was black and curled around his sneering lips. He looked to be in his late thirties.

The big man in the lead was in his fifties with a square face and heavy brows, his wide mouth set in a sneer that twisted his heavy black beard. He had to weigh over two hundred pounds and had arms the size of railroad ties.

"The big one's Fontane," Ricky whispered. "The fancy one's Trace. The one with the crooked nose is Switz. I don't know the other."

The men reined up near the camp, and Trace was fixing his black eyes on Will, taking his measure. Will knew of this man, a hired killer without honor.

Fontane had a Winchester repeater resting across the pommel as he growled, his nostrils flaring.

"You McBrides are a little far south, ain't you?"

Ricky sat cross-legged and sipped his coffee as he grinned up at the man. "You sure do look mean, Fontane. I hope

Walker pays you plenty."

"Mr. Walker to you, McBride."

Slowly, deliberately, Will stood up. "There's a lady present, mister. And you ain't tipped your hat."

"Who the devil are you?"

"Will Tanner," Ricky said.

Fontane's mouth twisted tight, and it took him a long time to respond, his little eyes gleaming. Will had seen that look in the other men he had hunted. And Fontane's voice became deep and husky.

"The bounty hunter? Well, I ain't scared of you, Tanner. No matter how many notches you got on that gun. So you just get out of my way. And I mean, right now."

"You ain't tipped your hat," Will said. "You gonna make me?"

Will moved slowly toward him, and Fontane lifted the rifle to aim it at Will's chest. The man was confident, sneering. He was bigger and looked mean as sin, his beady eyes narrowed.

Suddenly Will lunged, seizing the rifle and yanking it sideways, pulling Fontane half out of the saddle as his horse shied. Then Will grabbed the man's bandanna and jerked him clean out of his seat, throwing him sideways toward the ground like a sack of wheat.

Fontane managed to seize Will's arm and pull him down with him. Fontane was bigger and stronger, but he was awkward, and Will slammed his fist into the man's face, flattening his nose, then pounded his belly. Fontane gasped, clawing at him and missing.

Will jumped to his feet, and Fontane stumbled up-ward, bellowing and charging like a mad bull, but Will hopped aside like a rabbit, and the big man staggered past.

Fontane turned in fury, and Will hit him again and again, darting around him. Fontane wasn't fast enough to land his blows, except one glancing blow to the jaw, which snapped Will's head back and stunned him. Will got him again in the belly, his fist sinking deep. Fontane dropped to his knees, fighting for breath, eyes round.

Will took the man's hat and sent it sailing toward the creek where it disappeared into the chasm.

"Next time you're around a lady, tip your hat," Will said grimly. Then he turned away, fighting to breathe again. He hurt from the blow Fontane had managed to land on his jaw, his neck nearly having snapped, and his fists hurt from his own strikes.

"Look out!" Ricky shouted.

TWO

Will jumped aside as his right Colt leaped into his hand, and he was ready to fire, but Fontane had just cleared the holster and his six-gun was still pointed downward. The big man stared at Will's weapon in blank dismay. He slowly put his gun away and got clumsily to his feet, still gasping for air, his dirty face reddening.

"Now get out of here," Will said. "You're interruptin' our breakfast."

Fury was turning Fontane even redder as he picked up his Winchester and struggled to mount his horse. Still breathing hard, he turned in the saddle, glaring down at Will as he wiped his receding hairline with the back of his hand.

"You're a dead man, Tanner."

"I want to see the rest of them hats move."

Two of the three riders with Fontane hesitated, but as they stared at Will's dark burning eyes, they slowly tipped their hats to Darcie McBride. It took a lot longer for Trace to smile and lift his hat. Then the four of them turned and rode west along the river.

Will drew a deep breath, then turned to see the McBrides grinning from ear to ear. He shrugged and waited until the riders were out of sight, then sat down to refill his cup. He was hurting, dirty, and drenched with sweat.

"Wow," Ricky said. "I never seen anyone draw so fast. How come I never heard of you? Are you really a bounty hunter? Are you after somebody? It sure seems like Fontane knew of you, all right. Sure scared him plenty. He's gonna be mad, so watch out. He holds a grudge. And he sure wouldn't mind bushwhacking you. You really got notches on your gun?"

"No."

"Did you see ole Trace lookin' you over? He's a real killer they say. But he sure didn't take you on. And after he seen you draw, maybe he won't even try. But ole Switz, he's too dumb to do anything right."

Darcie was smiling. "Thank you, Mr. Tanner."

"Will."

"Is that for William?"

He shrugged, a little embarrassed. "No."

"Can I guess?" she persisted. "Will you tell me if I'm right? Is it Wilford? Willard? Wilhelm?"

"Wilmer?" Ricky added.

Will shook his head. "Forget it."

"Someday I'll figure it out," she said. "But after we have a little more coffee, we have to get back. Walker's men are getting too bold."

Ricky nodded. "When Pa was murdered three years ago, we had to sell off the land east of Tonto Creek to Walker. We kept the foothills. But if we could ever find Pa's gold mine, we'd be all right."

Darcie sipped her coffee, then spoke softly. "Our folks met during the war when she was working in a hospital and he was wounded. Then they came out here, leaving us behind until they could settle. Right after, gold was struck up on Yellow Mountain."

"By the time Darcie and me got here, they'd had Toby. Pa was murdered right after, and we never found out who done it. But Walker could have paid to have it done, just to get Mom and the ranch. He's a lawyer and real smooth, been after Mom all along. And his nephew Skip tried to get Darcie, but she wouldn't have 'im."

Darcie refilled their cups. "They started their own town north of the river and called it Walkersville."

"Any law out here?"

Ricky shook his head. "Not unless you count Sheriff Pike in Walkersville. Walker pinned a badge on him without no election. Nobody argued. And we ain't a state yet. I know there's a U.S. Marshal somewheres, but we ain't seen 'im."

"We wrote a letter to Denver," she said. "We received a polite answer, and that's about it."

"Trace is a hired killer," Ricky added. "And Pike has a couple gunmen that wouldn't win any popularity prizes. And then there's Domino. Owns the gambling hall. They say he won it at cards. Looks like a dude, but he's got crazy eyes."

Will was right interested. "How far to town?"

"You keep followin' the river west. You'll get there by sundown," Ricky said. "And we'd sure like it if you came to see us. You just ride past town and head west along the river until you get to Tonto Creek, then turn north along the foothills. Seen a lot of mule deer, still got their horns. You and me, we could go hunting. Leave the women at home."

Darcie gave him a push, and he laughed, then took her hand and pulled her to her feet.

Will stood up, pushing his hat back from his brow.

He watched them gather their mounts and make ready to leave. They waved at him as they forded the river downstream and disappeared over the hill.

For a long moment Will could not move. He had basked in an hour or more of joy, laughter, and youth. And now the silence was broken only by the hum of the river. He had never felt so alone and sad.

Staring into the campfire, pain rumbled through him as repressed memory came barreling forth like a cannon ball, hitting him square in the chest.

Eight years ago. It was eight painful years ago that a laughing, golden haired, blue-eyed young woman with a six-week-old, blue-eyed son in her arms was taken to town by her neighbors to see the doctor for a checkup and to order supplies for the Tanner's shirttail outfit, while he had stayed to work the ranch.

Will had been only twenty, but every inch a man. Cattle and horses had been his life, until he had met Jenny. They had started a spread near Pecos Junction, Texas, and their child was born one year after the wedding.

But that fateful day, the neighbor and his wife had returned alone with painful news.

"Your wife was alone on the wagon," he had said. "The Grissom gang must have sauntered into the express office unnoticed before covering their faces. Shots were fired inside, and them fellas came chargin' out with sacks in one hand and six-shooters in the other. A dozen of 'em. But the town reared up and was shootin' like crazy."

Choking back his tears, the old man had continued. "The wife and I were inside the store. When them Grissoms saw they was in trouble, one of 'em grabbed your wife off the wagon seat and pulled her across his saddle. She wouldn't let go of the baby. Folks had to stop shootin'. A posse was got up and took off after 'em, but they lost 'em."

Will was a good tracker, and one day he had found the grave down along the Rio Grande at Big Bend. A crude wooden cross tied together with her favorite initialed scarf, and the baby's bonnet still dangling from it. Someone had etched WOMAN AND CHILD, PECOS JUNCTION on the wood.

A dead horse lay nearby at the foot of the ridge.

Tears stung his eyes as he remembered wanting to go into the grave for her locket with the only portrait of her and his son, but he had been unable to bring himself to do so.

From what he could see by the signs, her horse had fallen with her from the ridge. Yet only one man had come down to bury her. One man on foot, bootprints left in the hardened mud.

With practice, Will had become a machine with lightning draw, emotions sealed, until the McBrides had come to tear down the wall he had built around himself.

But the McBrides didn't know why he had come.

In mid-afternoon, Ricky and Darcie McBride returned to their ranch. They unsaddled by the main corral. There were sheds and smaller enclosures where other horses stood tossing their heads and nickering. They could see smoke curling from the single level ranch house set in the grove of aspens north of where they stood.

Beyond, the foothills rose in scattered forest of yellow pine, spruce, juniper, and aspens. A red-tailed hawk sailed overhead like a bullet and disappeared over the hill.

"Don't you think he was handsome?" she asked.

"Who? That hungry old hawk?"

She poked at him. "You know who I mean. Will Tanner."

"Well, maybe, in an ugly sort of way."

"I hope he doesn't go to work for Walker."

"He will. That kind always does."

She frowned, and while Ricky went to grain the horses, she went up through the aspens to the house that sat on a rise, a long rambling building with stove and fireplace and thick rugs that were their mother's pride. Rifles were on the wall and in a rack, and a worn guitar hung on a hook.

Maggie McBride greeted her. Darcie flipped her hat onto a wall hook and turned. "Hi, Mom. We sure are hungry."

Her mother, a sweet-faced, rather lovely, blue-eyed, graying red-headed woman in her forties, who was full of figure and rather short, wearing an apron over her calico dress, smiled and hugged her.

"Darcie, you smell like a horse."

Toby had been kneeling where he had just stacked an armload of wood by the fire, and, he got to his feet, his clothes dusty from the shed. He was tall for his nine years, his dark hair unkempt, dark brown eyes large and filled with delight, his cheekbones high and rosy.

"That's Darcie all right, Mom. Smelly."

Darcie laughed and told them about Will Tanner and how

he handled Fontane. "He sure was handsome. He's got big shoulders and—"

"Darcie, that's not seemly."

"Why not? It'd be all right if I was talking about a horse, so why not a man?"

Toby grinned. "You're acting silly, Darcie."

When the boy went outside, Darcie turned to her mother. "How did you get Pa, Mom?"

"What?"

"How did you catch Pa?"

Maggie blushed. "Why, honey, after he was all healed up, he was courting me."

"I know, but what pushed him over the edge?"

"Well, I shouldn't tell you, but I fell and pretended to be hurt, and when he picked me up in his arms, he got all flustered and, well, then we got married and had three children."

"That's all it took?"

"Now you never mind, Darcie."

While the McBrides settled in for the evening, Will Tanner was riding north toward the town of McBride. His path took him through a stand of aspens and pines, high above the creek and on a narrow trail. Bluebirds sang in the branches, and a squirrel darted out of sight.

And a bullet slammed into Will's back.

THREE

Will spun his horse and tried to stay in the saddle, but the bullet had struck his left upper back near his neck and had shot clean through the flesh, leaving blood running down his shirt. It stung like blazes. He grabbed the horn with his left hand and pulled his Winchester with his right. His black was nervous, tossing its head.

Low on the saddle, Will kept his horse moving. He feared he would never get back astride if he fell off. As he neared the edge of the trees, he reined up and turned in the saddle, but he saw nothing.

Was it Fontane getting revenge? Had someone followed him from El Paso? Was Will the tracker or the prey?

He stayed at the edge of the trees as his dark eyes scanned the open country ahead of him. To his right was the river winding its shallow way eastward with cottonwoods along its path. Green hills rolled in all directions with scattered pines and aspens. To the west, he could see the distant blue of the snowcapped mountains. It was late afternoon under a clear sky.

Pain was shooting through his upper back and to his neck, the blood having slowed as shock wore off and pain set in, leaving him drenched with sweat as he shoved his bandana inside his shirt to cover the front of the wound.

It was twilight as he rode into McBride, a neat little, quiet town south of the river. A wooden bridge was to the north where it crossed over to a wagon road and the larger town of Walkersville.

Will headed for the lights of the small, two-story hotel on the east side of the street, set between a store and the town hall. Across the street was another store with boots hanging outside, a gunsmith, and the smithy and livery, with scattered houses behind them.

The only horses on the street were two fuzzy bay geldings in front of the hotel, and a bearded man with a round nose, likely in his eighties, was sitting on the bench near the entrance. Will saw no one else on the street as he slid his Winchester into the scabbard.

He reined up, leaning on the pommel as the old man stood up and came forward. Will slowly stepped down from the saddle. He was dizzy from loss of blood, but he managed to reach the railing and wrap the reins around it.

"You need help, son?"

"Shot in the back."

The old man came down to take his arm. "Lean on me. No doctor around here, but old Elmer's inside. He's a retired horse doctor, older then me even, but he can help you just the same. My name's Timothy."

"Will Tanner."

"The bounty hunter?"

"That's what they say."

"Well, it don't matter none. You need help."

Will slid his arm around the man's shoulder, towering above him but grateful for the help. They went inside the small, empty hotel lobby where there were two couches set near the hearth of a blazing fire. No one was at the counter. In the back, stairs led to the second floor, and there was a cafe off to the right of them. Will could smell the hot coffee as he slumped on one of the couches.

"You stay put, young fella. I'll get Elmer."

Elmer was in his nineties, a small man with big eyes and nose, but he was friendly enough and was able to not only stop the bleeding but also to administer a good bandage.

"You lost a lot of blood, but the bullet went clean through and didn't do any damage. You'll be all right. You just need a day's rest to get yourself back together. You got any idea who done it?"

"Had a run-in with a fellow named Fontane. Reckon I made him mad. Could be he followed me."

"Well, you get some rest," Timothy said. "We'll take care of your horse and bring in your gear. And we'll get you a room."

With Elmer and Timothy checking on him and bringing light food, Will rested a day and a night. But the second night of his stay, he insisted on joining them in the empty hotel cafe.

Despite having his left arm in a sling, he enjoyed a good steak with beans and wonderful coffee. He pushed his hat back as he downed another cup of coffee and the men told him about the rowdy Walkersville and the quiet McBride.

"Only excitement this side the river," said Elmer, "is lookin' for the new Montgomery Ward catalog."

Timothy sipped his coffee. "Ain't just McBride. Except for

foul places like Walkersville, things is gettin' civilized. And the Indians are gettin' pushed in every direction.

"Denver newspaper says General Crook is marching up through Wyomin' Territory. Going to round up the Sioux and Cheyenne, just so them miners can clean out the Black Hills. Got that fancy Custer up there with 'im. I figure they's bit off more'n they can chew. I'd say ole Sittin' Bull and Crazy Horse have been pushed too far."

"Yeah, with buffalo bein' wiped out for their hides at three dollars a crack," Elmer said. "And Colorado's about to be a state. Makes a man want to keep movin'. I'm thinkin' of headin' for Alaska."

Timothy laughed. "No gold up there. Just ice and snow and them big white bears."

They talked on about politics and the pending election. As Will listened to them, he felt peaceful. This was the way a man's life should be, sitting with old timers and listening, having a good hot cup of coffee.

When Elmer retired for the evening, Timothy looked around the empty cafe. "Now you're feelin' better, maybe you can tell me why you come to McBride."

Will shrugged. "I'm lookin' for a man named Hank Grissom. And four of his friends."

"I know everybody," Timothy said. "I don't know no Grissom. But wait. Yeah, Hank Grissom. Wasn't that the Reb guerilla about eight years ago that refused to surrender and went to robbin' and killin'? Bad ones, they was. I thought they was all dead. You know what they look like?"

"No."

"Big reward on them?"

Will shrugged. "Years ago there was, but I'm not after 'em for that."

"Personal, huh?"

Will nodded. "What do you know about Walker?"

"He's awful slick and right greedy. And he was after Maggie McBride even afore her man was murdered."

"You think Walker killed him?"

"We never found out who done it, but seein's how Walker bought out half their ranch and ain't gonna rest until he gets Maggie and the rest of it, it makes you wonder."

"But McBride has three children."

"Walker's a lawyer. He'll take care of them in short order, and they won't get nothin', you can bet on it. And he already owns half the valley and most of the town across the river. His freight line brings gold down from the stamp mill. His express company controls everything that goes in and out over there."

Will downed another swallow of hot coffee. "Maybe I'll have a look at this Walker."

"Nab, he ain't your man. Too much of a dude. Anyhow, lawyers got their hands in your pocket legal like. You'd best be lookin' at the likes of Pike and a couple gunmen he's got, and Fontane. And some of them mean ones like Trace. And yeah, maybe Domino."

"Runs the gambling hall?"

"Slick dude. With crazy eyes. Just lookin' at 'im, you can tell he'd slit your throat for a dollar."

"You was sayin' how you ran a store. You got a shirt to fit me?"

Timothy leaned back. "You bet. Got everything from frilly bonnets and stomach bitters to button shoes and plug tobacco.

Carryin' a big account for the McBrides. Before he got killed, their old man would come in with a little pinch of gold dust. Real pure stuff. Probably why he's dead. He was beat up pretty bad afore they shot 'im."

Later that night in his room, as he lay on the bed fully dressed, staring at the black spider on the ceiling, Will wondered if he was going to die before he ever found Grissom.

In the morning, after breakfast, Will checked out of his room, his left arm still in a sling, and walked into the morning sunlight with Timothy. They took his gear to the livery and saddled his horse.

"The men I'm lookin' for won't be in McBride," Will said.

"I'm no gun hand, so you're on your own. But I can tell you this, you run up against Sheriff Pike, you'd better watch yourself. He's big as a grizzly and looks like one."

"And he's the only law around here?"

Timothy nodded. "Yeah, except a miner's court up on Yellow Mountain. Now Pike, he has a couple hot shot gunmen named Prudo and Packard always hangin' around. Walker pays all three of 'em."

Will thanked him, then rode across the wide wooden bridge that was some twenty feet across and plenty weathered. The river was shallow here and icy clean with streaks of white water around the rocks.

As he rode north into Walkersville, he saw a lot of horses and mules at the railings. To his left was another smithy and livery, sheriff's office, several stores, an express office with a stage notice out front, and a miner's hall. On the right were two large saloons, a gambling hall named the Golden Wheel, a cafe and a miner's hotel. One building that said newspaper was boarded up, making it clear there was no free speech in Walker's town.

It was still midmorning and plenty quiet.

Will reined up in front of the express office and dismounted. Leaving his horse at the railing, he adjusted his sling and walked onto the boardwalk, read the notice about the stage having just left and looked inside, seeing a counter and a lot of notices posted on the wall.

There was a pretty woman in her late twenties sitting on a chair just inside the door. She was wearing a red velvet dress and smiling at him. He tipped his hat and backed into the sunlight as a rough voice growled in his ear.

"You want somethin', mister?"

Slowly, Will, who was nearly six feet, turned to look up at a man with huge shoulders and a thick, short neck. Wearing a cowhide vest with a badge on it, the man had an ugly face, crooked teeth, a sneer that would tum most men yellow, and little dark eyes.

"I'm Pike. The sheriff of this here town."

"Will Tanner."

The beady eyes became hot burning coals, and Pike's mouth twisted with sour disdain. "Yeah, the bounty hunter. What happened to your arm?"

"Bushwhacked on the way into town."

"See who it was?"

"Nope."

"Well, my jurisdiction's only to the town limits, so I can't do nothin'. Whatta you want around here?"

"Hank Grissom."

"Ain't nobody here by that name."

"What happened to the newspaper?"

Pike grunted. "Editor was strung up."

Will studied him a moment, then got on his horse and rode across the street. He could feel the man's gaze burning a hole in his back. Maybe Pike had just beard of Will's reputation. Or maybe he had something to hide.

Will dismounted in front of the cafe and draped the reins over the railing.

A farmer's wagon was pulling into town and to a halt in front of the miner's hotel next to the cafe. There were sacks of produce in the bed. The bearded, wrinkled man, who appeared to be in his eighties, was talking to himself, but he saw Will and raised his hand.

"Hey, there, young fella. Tie up my horses, will yuh?"

Will took the lead rope in his right hand and tied it loosely to the railing. Then he found himself helping the old man down. There was a black hound in the wagon bed lying on the sacks, its nose stuck over the side, too lazy to move, eyes half closed.

"Name's Grady. That old hound is Fred. Got me some peaches across the valley. Everyone says I'm crazy, but they sure pay in gold when we bottle 'em up."

"Will Tanner."

"Let me buy you some coffee, Will."

Inside, Grady said he was a widower but had family in Missouri. And he had nothing good to say about Walker or his men. "I don't trust any of 'em. But everyone leaves me alone. I got peaches, melons and some hogs, and a dozen hens. You can bet they all want what I got."

"What's this Walker look like?"

"Grey hair, in his forties. Handsome fellow. Dresses real

fancy. And mighty arrogant. His nephew Skip's just like him. Now I hear Skip's fiance already come in on the stage and is waitin' over at the express office."

Will nodded. "I saw a woman over there."

"I hear she's from some high-tone family. Them kind all stick together, you know."

After a hot cup of coffee with the old man, Will was the first to leave the cafe, but he had barely stepped onto the boardwalk when he was faced with two of the nastiest and most arrogant looking gunmen he had ever seen.

FOUR

The two men blocked Will's exit from the cafe. They were in their late twenties, one big and heavy of build with big hands, the other skinny and average height. They wore leather vests and tied down holsters. Their hats were shoved back, revealing the curly brown hair on the skinny one and matted blond hair on the other. They had smooth faces and thin noses. Both were old enough to have ridden with Grissom.

The skinnier man spoke with a twang. "You're in my way, mister."

Will stepped aside, but the heavier youth quickly moved in front of him. "Now you're in my way."

"Look, I'm just a stranger in town."

"I'm Prudo," said the skinny one, "and this is my friend Packard."

"Will Tanner."

"Yeah, and we heard about you leavin' graves all over Texas. You ain't welcome around here. We got us a peaceable town, and we aim to keep it that way."

"You calling me out?"

The two men shook their heads. They were not going to be fair about this. By the look in their beady eyes, Will knew he was in for it.

"We ain't drawin' on you, Tanner," Prudo said. "We're just gonna beat you to a pulp."

"Two to one?"

Packard, the heavier one, slowly unbuckled his gun belt and handed it to his companion. "Only takes one, Tanner. I'm gonna squeeze the devil out of you and pound your face in."

Grady objected. "You takin' on a one-armed man?"

Packard promptly wrapped his left arm behind his back, hooking his thumb in his belt behind him. "Now it's even."

"This man's been wounded," Grady argued.

Prudo stepped aside, and Packard backed into the street, right hand lifted in readiness.

Still a bit weak and his back hurting, Will swallowed hard. He was aware that the boardwalks were becoming populated. Sweat was cold on his back.

He knew there was little chance of his winning a fight with this man, but he didn't figure he had any choice. He could pull his six-shooter, but somewhere in the crowd would be a rifle aimed at his gut, just waiting for an excuse to pull the trigger.

Will wasn't as afraid of dying as he was of having his hunt cut off before he could find Grissom.

He walked into the street, facing the big man. It was a warm day with no wind. Cold sweat was trickling down Will's rear, and his throat had never been so dry.

Packard was snickering, his big right hand swaying up and down. Will danced around a little, and Packard swung, missing. Will's right fist jabbed at the man's gut. Packard lowered his fist to protect himself, and his jaw fell right into Will's sudden upright jab, snapping his head back.

Will pounded the man's face, then darted away. He wasn't making a dent. His only chance was the belly. Packard roared and rushed him, but Will danced aside.

"Stay put, you little rooster."

Packard rushed again, and Will sidestepped near the nervous team of horses. Packard's fist blew hot wind past Will's face. Will backed toward Grady's wagon. When Packard charged, Will jumped aside and pushed him hard, and the man's head crashed into the bed. There was a loud crackling sound as the boards split. Fred the hound just stuck his head over the side, had a look, then went back to sleep.

Stunned, Packard dropped to his knees with a grunt.

Will backed away. Packard tried to rise, then dropped back down to his knees, shaking his head.

Convinced it was over, Will turned and walked back to the boardwalk where Grady was waiting.

"He didn't lay a hand on you," Grady said with a grin.

"Hold it, Prudo," said a cold voice from behind them.

Will spun, seeing Prudo, standing back by the cafe, slowly lowering his six-gun. Packard was down on the ground, holding his head. And coming from the shadow of the gambling hall was a man in a black coat and hat with a little string tie and red velvet vest. About fifty, he looked like a riverboat gambler, but he was holding an Army Colt in his right hand.

Prudo holstered his gun with a snarl. "You stay out of this, Harriman."

It was then that Pike got around to coming across the street. While Prudo went to help Packard, Pike stood with his thumbs in his gun belt and glared at Harriman, who slowly holstered his six-gun under his black coat. Pike's lips curled back from his teeth as he spoke.

"Tanner, you're wearin' out your welcome. And so are you, Harriman. We don't need gunfighters or professional gamblers in this town."

"You got no handbills on me," Will said. "I ain't leavin' until I find Grissom."

"And I'm not leaving," Harriman said, "as long as there's gold coming down the mountain."

"Just don't step out of line," Pike warned.

Pike turned to help Prudo walk the dazed Packard over to the sheriff's office. The crowd gradually dispersed.

Grady grinned and spoke under his breath. "Sure was worth comin' to town to see that. You fellas ever want to come out to visit, you come on. Just head past McBride's. You'll see my trees, all right."

Will was quiet a long moment, watching the old man climb into his wagon and drive toward the town of McBride, Fred's nose stuck over the side. Then he turned to Harriman. "Thanks for covering my back."

"Never liked them fellas."

"You're a professional gambler?"

"Right off the Mississippi. But I'm doing better here. These miners are not very good at cards. Of course, they lose most of it at Domino's Golden Wheel. When it spins, nobody wins, I can tell you that."

They moved back into the shade in front of the cafe, and Will adjusted his sling as he sat wearily on the bench. "What do you know about Domino?"

"Turn around and take a look. There he is, standing outside his place."

Slowly, Will turned. Some twenty feet away stood an evil looking man with near white eyes under dark, heavy brows. In his forties, he had a handsome face with a short black beard and mustache. With diamond studs and a gold watch chain, a fancy red vest and small-brimmed black hat, he seemed to be dressing in contrast to his real nature.

And the man really did have crazy eyes, as if he had no eyes at all, just white diamonds.

Now he was coming toward them.

"That was quite a show, Mr.—?"

Harriman smiled. "Tanner. Will Tanner. And this is Domino."

Domino's demeanor turned hostile, his pale eyes narrowed to slits, yet he was smiling all the while, and his sinister voice was deep. "The bounty hunter."

"Where are you from, Domino?" Will asked. The man snickered. "No one in this town is going to answer any of your questions, Mr. Tanner."

And with a slight bow, Domino turned and crossed the street to where Pike and the others were waiting.

"What do you know about Domino?" Will asked.

Harriman shrugged. "Not much. Everyone's afraid of him, and he likes it that way."

"But you're not afraid."

Harriman smiled, pushing his hat from his brow. "I think I can safely say I'm not afraid of anyone. Any' white man, that is. I've known a few Apache made my blood run cold."

"Know anything about Walker?"

"Sedge Walker? He's a lawyer. Owns half of Walkersville and a big ranch. Nephew named Skip, and there's Skip's fiance. Just came in on the stage."

Slowly, Will turned to see the young woman on the other side of the street. She was standing on the boardwalk with a feathered hat shading her eyes. Right pretty and maybe pushing thirty, she had the manner of a woman who thought everyone should kneel.

A wagon was coming down the street from the north.

"And there's Walker," Harriman said.

On the wagon seat was a man in his forties in a store-bought suit, his hat brim rather small, grey hair sleeked back. He was average size with heavy brows over pale brown eyes, a handsome man with strong features.

Riding behind him were two men. One was Fontane, and the other was a young version of Walker in his late twenties, well dressed with the same manner and heavy brows.

Harriman leaned on a post. "Skip Walker."

As the wagon approached, Walker slapped the reins to go a little faster, then reined up in front of the woman. Skip rode around the wagon, jumped down and bowed, then took her hands in his. It was obvious that kissing in public was not one of their weaknesses.

"Sweet, isn't it?" Harriman grunted.

Will stiffened as he realized the Walkers were heading for the cafe. As they came up closer, he saw that the girl had brown eyes and a flirtatious smile. He also noticed that Sedge Walker was fawning over her as he took one arm and Skip the other.

Harriman and Will tipped their hats, and the gambler smiled. "Good day, Mr. Walker."

The lawyer frowned, apparently not too thrilled to have his niece associating with a gambler, but he was polite.

"Mr. Harriman, may I present my nephew's fiance, Miss Eleanor Rutledge."

Harriman bowed. "Delighted. And this is Will Tanner."

Walker's gaze turned cold. "Yes, I heard about you, Tanner. I'm sure you'll understand if I do not present you to the lady."

Skip came forward, pushing his hat back as he looked Will over with a sneer. "You don't look so tough to me, Tanner."

Grim and unflinching, Will returned their stares and didn't move as the Walkers went inside the cafe. Eleanor looked over her shoulder, still smiling.

Harriman grinned. "You're not too popular."

"Reckon not."

"Still, Miss Eleanor was givin' you the eye."

"I got no time for women."

"Well, I was headin' out to McBride's to see about a horse they got for sale. Be gettin' there by sundown. And I hear Mrs. McBride is not only a pretty woman but a right fine cook. Why don't you ride along? Give your wound a chance to heal."

Will considered him carefully, trying to take his measure. The man was friendly enough, and he seemed straightforward, but Will had learned never to trust anyone. Still, he'd been shot once already. Having another man along might keep the bushwhacker at bay for a while.

"Sure you want to be associated with me?"

Harriman pulled his hat down tight. "I ain't one bit scared."

Will had to smile briefly. Although he preferred his solitude, riding with Harriman was little enough sacrifice if it would keep him alive until he found Grissom.

Harriman had his sorrel gelding already saddled at the livery with his bedroll behind the cantle. With Will on his black horse, the two men rode west along the north bank of the Little Rocky River.

Back at the cafe, an agitated Walker was holding his coffee cup in both hands. "I'm sorry, Eleanor. Harriman's respectable enough, but not that Will Tanner. I didn't like you being exposed to him."

"Come now. I've met all kinds of men back east. They're all alike, you know."

Walker frowned. "This is serious, Eleanor. Will Tanner is a killer. A bounty hunter. He's left bodies all over Texas."

Skip leaned back in his chair with a lazy smile. "He doesn't look that dangerous to me. I could take him easy."

"Men like that don't look to the right or left," Walker advised. "Nothing will stop them head on, but they do get it in the back."

Eleanor was pouting. "I don't want to talk about it anymore. I want Skip to say he's glad I'm here."

Skip looked around the empty cafe, then reached over and squeezed her hand. "When we get to the ranch, I'll show you how glad I am to see you. But not here among the peasants."

She smiled. "That's what I like about you, Skip. You're so wicked."

"Maybe I am at that," Skip said, grinning. "Say, Uncle Sedge, didn't I tell you this woman was gorgeous?"

Sedge was looking her over time and again. "Yes."

"Honey, Uncle Sedge here, he's been courtin' a widow lady. Maggie McBride. Not well educated and has no social position. But she has a ranch he's bound to get his hands on."

"Really, Sedge," she scolded. "A fine gentleman like you could have any woman you wanted. You should have a fine lady from a good family."

Skip laughed. "Sedge found out McBride was usin' pure gold to pay his bill at the store. I mean, high grade dust. Better than anything on Yellow Mountain. Now McBride's dead, but the gold's there somewhere. He figures the widow knows where it is."

Walker downed his coffee, looked Eleanor over once more, and then left to go across to the express office. Skip looked around to be sure the waiter was in the kitchen.

"My uncle's sure taken with you."

"Now, Skip, don't start that again."

"But I'm glad you're here, Eleanor."

"Yes, but your uncle looks in fine health to me."

"Fine health and stingy."

"But you wrote you were getting your inheritance early."

"Just have a little patience, honey."

"I don't plan to live in a dirty place like this, you know. There's no opera house. No fine clothing stores. Nothing but dirt and grimy old men."

"I guess you noticed how Sedge was looking at you."

"Oh, Skip, you're always so jealous."

"All men look at you that way. And I think you invite it. In fact, maybe you're thinkin' you'd be better off marryin' Sedge and gettin' the money firsthand."

She smiled, her hand in his. "Should I do that?"

His hand closed like iron on her fingers, and she squealed. When he saw the waiter looking from across the room, he released her hand and appeared contrite.

35

"Eleanor, just be patient. He's after McBride's gold, and I intend to get my hands on it. One way or another."

FIVE

William and Harriman rode west along the wandering, glistening Little Rocky River. It was a sunny afternoon, but there was a chill in the air. The green, rolling land was set with yellow flowers, fluttering birds still trying to mate but scattering as a golden eagle circled in the sky.

"I smell rain," Will said, adjusting his sling.

"Look, that's got to be Tonto Creek. We're supposed to follow it north until we see the trail to the ranch."

Will glanced at him as they turned along the narrow rocky stream. "Why do you need another horse?"

"Man always needs another mount, just in case."

"They had horses at the livery."

"A bunch of jugheads. Besides, I kept hearing about Maggie McBride. I want to see what she looks like. Women are scarce out here. And you know, a man in my profession gets tired as time goes on. I wouldn't mind settling down."

Will glanced at him and shook his head. "That's not it."

Harriman shrugged. "You're a curious man."

"So why do you want to go to McBrides?"

"Why are you hunting the Grissoms?"

"I got my reasons."

"I've been to Texas, Will. I know what happened to your wife and son."

"How do you know?"

"Was told about it in Pecos Junction. They don't mention your wife and son in the dime novels. I've got one in my saddlebags. Want to see it?"

"I've seen 'em."

"Makes you out to be a real terror. But whoever wrote 'em didn't know what made you a bounty hunter. They just make out that you're some kind of hero ridding the West of outlaws."

Before they reached the McBride ranch in the foothills, it clouded up, and they pulled out their leather jackets from behind their saddles. By the time they rode up to the corrals, it was drizzling rain, so they pulled on their slickers.

They found Ricky McBride at the barn, grinning.

"Sure glad to see you. We don't get much company."

Leaving the horses at the corral, Will and Harriman carried their saddlebags and gear, walking with Ricky up toward the house where smoke was curling from the chimney. The rain was dark and heavier now, beating at them and pouring off their slickers. They bent their heads as water swirled off their hat brims. Ricky kept looking at the gambler.

"I heard about you, Mr. Harriman. They say you never lose at cards."

"I'm just lucky, son."

"Mom's makin' us some beef stew tonight. And Darcie's makin' biscuits. The best darn biscuits you ever tasted. Big and fluffy."

Will felt his mouth watering, while inside the house, Darcie was blowing a strand of red hair off her face. She had flour on her nose and chin and all over her apron, which did not fully protect her shirt and riding skirt.

"Mom, you know I'd rather be outside."

"Darcie, you'll never get married if you don't practice your cooking. Men don't want to marry another cowhand."

"A servant, that's what they want."

Maggie, wearing a gingham dress with an apron, her graying hair drawn back from her pretty face, was smiling.

"Darcie, don't you know there's more to being a wife than cooking and sewing or raising children? Your father and I were like a team of horses. If you don't pull together, you don't get anywhere."

"So I'll take care of the cattle, and he can cook."

Maggie had to laugh. "What am I going to do with you? First you're telling me all about this Will Tanner, and now you're acting like you just don't care."

"Well, I'm not getting married anyhow. There's not one man on this earth that can make me get all silly like the girls I've seen at the dances. Fawnin' and blinking their lashes, and sashaying around."

Toby, who had brought in more wood from the leanto, was stoking the fire and looked up with a grin.

It was then the door opened, and Ricky walked in, shaking the rain from his hat and tossing it on a hook as he kicked the door closed. He then pulled off his slicker, shook it out and hung it.

"Did you grain my horse?" Darcie asked.

"What for?"

She picked up a pie tin. "I'm going to bust your, head."

And then she paused, staring in dismay as the door swung open again. Will and Harriman came walking inside with their gear. Flustered, she hurriedly wiped at her face, putting even more flour on her cheeks by mistake. She reached back at her long flowing hair, trying to fluff it.

Maggie smiled at her. "Are you all right, Darcie?"

"Of course I am. But these men are trackin' rain in the house as usual."

Will and Harriman removed their hats and wiped their boots on the entrance rug, then pulled off their slickers.

Ricky introduced them to Maggie and Toby, who was setting the table and looking as happy as his brother and sister.

Will swallowed hard, for this boy looked the way his son might have, except for the brown eyes. His child had bright blue eyes. Yet this boy could have been his with his dark wavy hair and high cheekbones. Toby's features almost mimicked Will's.

Ricky helped put their gear in the boys' room, then guided them to chairs at the table. There was no fire in the hearth at the moment, but wood was stacked and ready. Will kept glancing at the boy.

Darcie's face was still pink. "What happened to your arm, Will?"

"Bushwhacked on the way into town."

"Bet it was Fontane," Ricky said. "He sure was mad when you whupped him."

Harriman turned to Will. "What's this about Fontane?"

Ricky told the story with embellishment.

Stew was steaming in a kettle on the iron stove, next to the

40

big coffee pot, and Darcie was sniffing the air. Her biscuits. She spun and grabbed a pot holder, then removed the biscuits, which were big and fluffy.

Harriman smiled. "Now those are biscuits. If I was ten years younger, I'd sure be courtin' you, Miss Darcie, but if that stew's as good as it smells, I think I'll be courtin' you, Maggie. How about it? Want to take an old bachelor in hand?"

Now it was Maggie's turn to blush and stumble around.

All through supper, Will had to fight to keep from staring at Toby. Was Will the only one who saw the resemblance? He glanced at Ricky, who was busy praising his young brother.

"Toby was the only one who could track down that old cow this morning. I bet he could out-track any old Indian."

Toby grinned. "Ricky used to try to hide from me, but I could always find 'im."

"It's a gift," Maggie said.

Will felt increasing sadness. He was a good tracker himself, and his own son would have learned in time.

The stew and biscuits were delicious. The peach pie was unbelievably good with a thick fluffy crust, and on top of that, the coffee was wonderful.

"I think I died and went to heaven," Harriman said.

"You'll both stay the night, of course," Maggie responded, her cheeks still rosy.

Toby stoked up the fire in the hearth. Rain and wind were beating at the house with a constant roar. The men sat around the crackling fire while the women cleared the table. It was then that Ricky prodded Harriman for details of life on the Mississippi. Toby sat cross-legged, listening in awe.

The more Harriman spun his tales, the more Will was

convinced the man was not a riverboat gambler, but he liked him and didn't care what his true background was. So long as he had never ridden with Grissom, that is.

Will and Harriman had been given the two leather chairs, and they slouched down, so comfortable they were ready to fall asleep. Ricky had pulled over one of the chairs from the table and was sitting between them.

Maggie insisted on looking at Will's wound and putting on a fresh bandage. "Now stop squirming, Mr. Tanner. I patched up a lot of men in the War Between the States."

Once Will's shirt was back in place, his face no longer so red, Darcie brought more coffee, then she and her mother sat on pillows on either side of the blazing hearth. Both women appeared flustered. Maggie told her dream of someday sending Ricky to Harvard and Darcie to nursing school in New York.

Darcie made a face. "Why not medical school?"

Ricky laughed. "A woman doctor? You'd scare 'em plenty. And me, if I go to Harvard, it'd be to play that rugby football."

"More like lawn tennis," she chided.

But it was obvious there was no money for school, and to take away the edge, Ricky took out his harmonica. He began to play lively tunes, and after awhile, the two women sang. Maggie had a pleasant voice, but Darcie had the high soprano. Toby joined in from time to time.

Will closed his eyes, listening to their songs. Harriman was lost in the words and music, his eyes misting. The women sang in unison, and it was beautiful to hear.

They sang about the Little Old Sod Shanty on My Claim, the Zebra Dun, and the old Chisholm Trail and of bad men and cowboys.

The women then served more coffee, and Will found himself staring up into Darcie's shining blue eyes.

"Maybe you men would rather talk," she said.

Harriman shook his head. "Not a chance."

Ricky began to play "Cowboy Jack," and as Darcie sang, the words were painful to Will, who stared into the fire with his eyes brimming, knowing the song's sad story of the lonely cowboy well. Yet her voice was so sweet it softened the words.

When Darcie saw Will's sad face, she cut the song short without the unhappy ending, and Will was grateful.

She got up from her pillow, turned to the wall and took down the guitar, then wiped it off and handed it to a surprised Will. It felt strange in his hands, and Ricky stopped playing as they all watched. Memories burned in Will's brain, and yet he could not put the guitar down.

"Play what you want to hear," she said.

Will fingered the strings. Before he could stop himself, he was tuning it. He tried not to think of the times he had serenaded his young bride.

He started with "Old Dan Tucker," followed by "Cotton Eyed Joe" and every lively tune he could think of, while Ricky played along with delight. Then they both wearied.

The music faded, and the women sat staring into the flames. Toby was curled up asleep near them. Harriman glanced at Will, and both men read in each other's gaze how pleasant this all was.

Then Will began to play an old tune from the War Between the States. Ricky picked up on the sorrowful song, but it was Harriman who knew the words, singing slowly in a low, deep voice as if he had surely been in the war and was remembering men he would see no more.

43

As Harriman sang with emotion and misting eyes of weary soldiers longing for peace, Will watched him carefully. If this was a professional gambler, he had come a long way from somewhere else. The song over, everyone clapped except Will, who still held his guitar.

"Why, Mr. Harriman," Maggie said. "You should be in a choir, if we had one, that is."

"Yeah," Ricky said with a grin. "The choir at the Golden Wheel."

Embarrassed, Harriman cleared his throat and changed the subject. "I looked at that bay you had for sale. What are you asking?"

Maggie smiled. "What are you willing to pay?"

"I'd like to try him out first."

That night, Will and Harriman slept on the floor in Ricky and Toby's room, their saddlebags and _gear beside them. Will lay there in the darkness a long time listening to the heavy rain before he slept.

He awakened before dawn to the smell of fresh coffee. Wind and rain were still rattling the roof and walls. Wooden windows were rattling. Harriman was in deep sleep, and Toby was curled up on his bunk, breathing softly.

Will put on his boots and hat in the pale light that was coming under the door, then strapped on his six-guns. He paused to look at Toby, and he knew his imagination had found more resemblance than was probably there.

Next to Harriman, from the flap of his saddlebag, a dime novel was exposed. Will grimly ignored it, hating every one of them.

Quietly, he left the bedroom and entered the front room

where a fire was blazing in the hearth, flames curling over chunks of pine and aspen, the scent rising strong and good. The only lamp that was lit was on the table. Most of the light in the room was from the hearth.

And standing by the stove was Darcie McBride, potholder in hand as she moved the coffee to the side. She was wearing her riding skirt and a white blouse, her long hair flowing about her shoulders. She turned to smile bashfully at him.

She poured fresh coffee for them, and they sat in leather chairs in front of the fire. It was nice and quiet for a long while, and she seemed content with the silence, looking serious. After a while, Will spoke softly.

"Those were mighty fine biscuits you made last night."

"Thank you."

"You have a good family."

"What about yours, Will?"

"I never knew my folks. They were killed by Comanches."

The walls shuddered in the wind, and Darcie leaned forward to be closer to the hot fire. "I'm sorry. How old were you?"

"Months old, I guess."

"But they didn't kill you."

He stared at the leaping flames, wondering why he was talking so much. "My folks had hidden me in the basement when the fighting started. They didn't find me, but I reckon they would have taken me for one of their own. My mother was a quarter Comanche as it was."

Darcie gazed at him curiously. His high cheekbones were no lie, and his black hair gave truth to his words.

"But why did they kill her then?"

"Man who found me, he read the signs. He said she fought

right alongside my father and killed some of them afore they got both of 'em."

"Who was this man that found you?"

"A drummer. Took me in. Named me. Even taught me my letters. Died when I was fourteen."

"And after that?"

"I fell in with some trail drivers. Started out as a wrangler. Ended up herdin' cows."

Will fell silent, staring into the flames. He had not talked this much in eight years. It was a long while before he glanced at her with his burning question.

"What about Toby?"

"My little brother?"

"You say your folks had him when they first settled here, before you and Ricky came out to join them?"

"That's right."

"So Maggie was Toby's mother."

"Of course. Why do you ask?"

"He doesn't look like any of you with your red hair."

"Toby takes after our great-grandfather, on my mother's side. None of us ever knew him, but Mom said he had dark hair and brown eyes, just like Toby. She said Toby's his spitting image."

Will shrugged and wiped his brow, and it was her turn to catch him off guard.

"Are you married, Will?"

"I was. She died eight years ago."

"I'm sorry."

Darcie stood up to get more coffee, but she tripped on the rug before she could get to the table. She gasped, called out and fell over backwards, landing on her rear and then lying flat, her hand on her face. She was stunned but not hurt.

Will jumped up and came around to kneel. "Are you all right?"

"Knocked the wind out of me."

"Can you get up?"

She thought a moment. "I don't think so." Certain she was faking, Will hesitated. Yet he'd be an idiot if he didn't lift her up in his arms. He slid his hands under her waist and behind her knees, lifting her gently. The effort pulled on his sore wound, but it was worth it.

She felt heavier than expected, but she felt mighty good. She was soft and warm and supple. As he lifted her into his embrace, her head rolled against his chest, and she slid her hand upward, clinging to his vest.

"Oh," she moaned.

"You are hurt," he said, carrying her to one of the big chairs.

As he set her down gently, her hands slid around his neck, pulling his face down toward hers. Startled, be was frozen as he stared into her shining blue eyes. He was bending over her, his hands on the chair arms, trying to rise, but she held him close.

And now her sweet rosy lips were pressed to his rough ones, and lightning bolts shot through him, clear to his toes, leaving him so weak he couldn't move. She kept kissing him, and he felt his whole world crashing around him. All the years of hate and vengeance, all the dreaded memories, everything, came tumbling down. Her fingers were cold at his hot neck, and he was crumbling.

And he kissed her back. And kissed her. And kissed her.

"My land." It was Maggie behind him.

Will reddened and Darcie's hands slid from his neck, but as she leaned back in the chair, her eyes were closed. Out of breath and a complete disaster, Will dragged himself away from her. As he straightened, he felt his body crack all over.

"She fell down," Will said, awkwardly.

Maggie came to check her daughter, feeling her hot face, but Darcie waved her away. "I'm all right, Mom."

For a moment, Maggie just looked from the embarrassed Will to Darcie's blush, and then she went over to the stove.

But Will was left shaken as he sat down in the chair' a few feet from Darcie. Staring into the hearth, he wondered if he had been kissing Darcie or an eight-year-old memory. His heart was still beating fast and loud in his chest, and he was falling apart.

He was glad when Harriman and Ricky joined them, but not so glad when Toby walked in holding the dime novel.

"Look what fell out of your bags, Mr. Harriman." And there in the firelight for all to see was the dime novel that declared: "Will Tanner, Scourge of the Plains."

Will paled, and Ricky took it in his hands.

"Hey, Will, you're some kind of hero. Look at this.

You brought in a whole bunch of bad guys. And you killed five men in gunfights."

"Six," Harriman said. "He just got Cory."

Everyone was staring at Will. He felt inches high. Looking at the women's wide-eyed gaze, he felt color 'rushing into his face. He glanced at Ricky's amazement and Harriman's amusement. But it was Toby who surprised him.

"Ah, it's all made up."

Maggie drew a deep breath. "Well, my oh my."

Ricky kept looking through the pages as he grinned. "It says here you're ridding the west of predators. You' re a stalwart defender of justice. You've brought in twenty wanted killers."

Darcie looked over Ricky's shoulder. "The drawing doesn't look much like you, Will."

Harriman grinned. "There are about six other Tanner novels out there."

It was then that Will, his face burning, reached for his hat. "I'm goin' down to check on my horse."

"Hurry back for breakfast," Maggie said.

Will was outside without his coat before he realized how icy it was and barely light. Although the sky was clear, it was mighty cold and damp, and his boots were sliding in the mud. As he started downhill toward the corrals, he heard the door slam again.

He paused, turning, hoping it was Harriman.

But it was Toby, in his shirt sleeves and hatless.

Frozen in his tracks and hurting clear through, Will watched the boy come after him. Toby's eyes were chocolate brown like Will's, but not like Will's infant son, whose eyes had been bright blue like his mother's. Yet the similarity in features was uncanny.

"Will, I'm right sorry."

"Sorry?"

"I mean, I've been thinkin', and now I figure you didn't want Mom and Darcie to see that novel. It was wrong of me to show it to 'em. Women are such sissies. They just don't understand that sort of thing."

Will swallowed hard. "I know."

"But I do. All them fellas you got was outlaws. But there's

more to it, ain't there? You ain't no real bounty hunter, I can tell. Some of 'em done somethin' bad to you, so you track 'em all down for revenge. Ain't that so?"

"Yes."

"And it says you only got some of that Grissom gang when you first started out, so maybe it was them, and you're still lookin' for the rest of 'em?"

Will nodded, disturbed by the boy's perception. Toby's eyes were rounder. "Are any of 'em here?"

"I don't know."

"Do you know what they look like?"

"No."

"That novel says that Grissom was the brains. So he'd be somebody smart, ain't that so?"

"Not necessarily. Look, you're freezing out here."

The boy wrapped his arms about himself and grinned. "Yeah, and Mom is goin' to get after me. And you, too."

Together, they started back up the trail to the house, and Will was sweating despite the chill. Back inside, they both headed for the hearth where Ricky had built up the fire. The women were cooking on the iron stove, and Harriman had returned his novel to his saddlebags.

Will glared at him and muttered under his breath. "You and I are goin' to have a serious talk when we leave here."

Harriman grinned. "I know."

While Will was trying to get hold of himself, Fontane was in town to see Pike, who had been awakened from his sleep in the sheriff's office, a one-room jail with one cell and an iron stove. There was a desk and board-covered windows.

Turning up the lamp, Pike pulled on his boots, annoyed at having been awakened, but Fontane was anxious.

"I tell you, Pike, I've seen bounty hunters before, but Tanner's got somethin' drivin' him, and he ain't gonna quit. We still got some big money on our heads."

"Let Prudo and Packard take care of him. They've got a hate on for him now."

Fontane grunted. "Those upstarts?"

"They've racked up a few notches."

"It's going to take a man to get rid of Tanner."

"Then you go ahead."

"I figured you bein' sheriff, you could get away with it."

"I don't figure we ought to do anything without checkin' with Grissom," Pike said with a yawn. "You know how he is, and I sure don't wanna cross 'im."

"I seen Tanner draw. He's too fast. It's goin' to take a bullet in the back."

"You tried that."

"He was too far away," Fontane said.

"Well, let's heat up the coffee and figure somethin'."

SIX

As Maggie was up at the house making fresh coffee for a noonday meal, Toby and Ricky were on the fence watching Harriman ride the bay horse around the largest corral. Darcie was leaning on the boards next to him, while Will was just inside the gate on foot, checking the bay out carefully.

"You got a winner," Will remarked.

Harriman grinned and backed up the bay, then spun it around twice. "Has an easy mouth, all right."

"Toby broke 'im," Ricky said. "It never even bucked."

Darcie laughed. "Except when Ricky got on it."

"Yeah," Toby said. "He nearly threw Ricky off."

"Ain't no horse can throw me," Ricky bragged. Later in the day when Will and Harriman were riding back toward town, following Tonto Creek under a dark, cloudy sky with the bay trailing on a lead rope, Will kept glancing at the easy-riding Harriman. When they reached the cottonwoods at the river, he reined up and twisted around in the saddle. Harriman grinned and pulled up beside him.

"All right, Harriman. Let's have it."

"What do you want to know?"

"You're no riverboat gambler."

"No."

"Are you a lawman?"

"Detective. Wells Fargo. I was hired by Jim Hume, Chief of Detectives, just for this job. Mostly, I was a peace officer, but Hume is mighty persuasive."

"And you're after Grissom?"

"We heard about Beeker's confession afore he died and how Grissom might be alive. And some of the stolen money might be around in some form or another. I've been tryin' to get to Grissom before you do. I hit El Paso right after you got Cory. Seems I just end up following you around. Never saw a man cover so much territory so fast."

"Your real name Harriman?"

"Yeah. But I'd appreciate it if this was just between us."

"Grissom and four of his men are all that's left."

"I know, but if we don't take 'em alive, I won't find any of the money. They made some big hauls. Wells Fargo likes to make recoveries. Good for business, you know."

"I don't care about the money."

"I'm sorry about your wife and son, but that was eight years ago, Will. You got to rejoin the living. Now take that Darcie McBride, she sure was flirting with you. When a nice girl like that sets her cap for a man, he's in trouble."

"I ain't fit for any woman."

"You'll find out you're wrong someday. And I hope it won't be too late. Pretty woman like that. And women so mighty scarce out here."

"Well, for a detective with a job to do, you were sure fawnin' over Maggie McBride. You had puppy dog eyes. If you'd had a tail, it would have been floppin' all over the place."

Harriman grinned. "Do you blame me?"

They paused as rain suddenly began to fall.

Rain that was already beating the roof of the Walker mansion. Inside, Sedge Walker was sitting at his desk in his den, working on his account books. The shelves behind him were stacked with law books, and paintings of Indians and cowboys decorated the walls as light filtered through velvet curtains.

Upstairs, Skip was standing in the hallway with Eleanor, who was wearing her red dress. He put his hands at her waist. "You sure look pretty, honey."

"Are you coming downstairs?"

"Nah, I want to sleep awhile. You go entertain Uncle Sedge. Maybe he'll just out and out give you the money."

"Hmm. Maybe I should marry him instead." Skip frowned. "What?"

"Honestly, Skip, you have no sense of humor."

"You know how jealous I am."

"But he's your uncle."

"Well, he won't be for long, and then we'll be rolling in money. We'll sell this place and go east where we belong, but you do anything funny, and I'll whip you."

"My, how vicious you are."

"And don't you forget it."

He kissed her passionately and went off to his room, while she fluffed her brown hair and went down the winding staircase to the plush parlor. She could see Sedge at his desk through the open door and she hesitated.

If she married that foolish, explosive Skip, it would only be for his inheritance, and it would involve bringing Sedge to an early demise. Worse, Skip could hang, and she could go to prison for the rest of her life. It would be damp and dingy and miserable.

But Sedge was still a young man, and there was a masculinity about him that wasn't forced, the way Skip's was. Skip had to constantly prove himself, while Sedge was so much a man, he had to do nothing.

If she married Sedge, she'd have it all, and there'd be no killing. She smiled at the thought, but she had no idea how Sedge felt about her. Yet.

She moved gracefully to the doorway of his office. "Oh, am I disturbing you, Sedge?"

He paused and leaned back in his chair, annoyed at first, but smiling as he took a good look at her, his pale eyes gleaming under his heavy brows.

"It's all right."

She entered the room and stood in front of his desk, allowing him to gaze at her womanly form and pretty face.

"Do you always: work, Sedge? Don't you ever play?"

"Such as?"

She smiled flirtatiously. "Whatever men do when they want to play out here."

"We hunt or fish."

"Is that all?"

He put his fingertips together. "If I wasn't so cynical, I'd think you were flirting with me."

"You are Skip's uncle, and I do want you to like me."

He ran his hand over his sleeked-back hair. "Not many women out here that look like you."

"Do I look better than Maggie McBride?"

He smiled thoughtfully. "Just different."

"You mean she's the motherly type."

"Yes."

"You want to marry a motherly type?"

Walker stood up slowly. "Where's Skip?"

"Asleep. Boys always sleep in the afternoon."

"What does that mean?"

"It means that men have other things to do."

"Dare I guess why you are here?"

"You're a lawyer. Can't you figure it out?"

He moved cautiously. "Why don't you show me what you have in mind?"

Eleanor didn't move as he came closer. She smiled at him, her brown eyes gleaming with invitation, and she drew a deep breath as his hands closed on her arms.

Now he was drawing her to him, and she could feel the pistol under his smoking jacket. He smelled like a man, and he was strong and big of shoulder.

And Sedge Walker was enamored of her perfume, the softness she gave so freely, the way her slim fingers went up around his neck.

"Maybe I oughta marry you myself," he muttered.

"Maybe you should."

"What about Skip?"

"He'll get over it."

Walker kissed her gently at first. Then hunger over-came him, and he was all over her, but she didn't resist and was kissing him back. Until they were interrupted by a shout.

"Blast you!"

Eleanor drew back as Sedge stiffened. They both turned, still in an embrace, and there in the doorway stood Skip Walker with his six-gun aimed at them. Eleanor turned cold with fear as Skip grimaced.

"I'll kill you both!"

"No, Skip," she pleaded.

Sedge thrust her away, jumped aside and pulled his pistol. Before Skip could pull the trigger, Sedge fired, and Skip gasped, eyes wide, a bullet in his chest as he staggered forward, firing into the floor, then collapsing in the doorway.

Eleanor cried out, her hand over her mouth.

Sedge moved a few steps forward, then stopped as he gazed down at his dead nephew. There was sweat on his face, and he wiped his brow with the back of his hand. He was shaking all over as he shoved his pistol back inside his coat.

It was then the front door swung open, and Fontane came hurrying inside, rifle cocked and ready, Trace on his heels. The men came to a halt near the entrance to Sedge's office, staring at Skip on the floor.

"What happened?" Fontane asked.

"He was cleaning his gun and shot himself."

"Yeah, sure looks like it."

"Get him out of here. Take him to the undertaker. We'll have the funeral tomorrow. Make sure everybody comes."

"What if anyone questions it?"

"Who's going to question me?"

"No one."

Trace wiped the snicker from his own face and pulled his hat down tight. "Looks like you won the prize."

Sedge Walker glared at him as Eleanor moved to his side, but Trace was a cold-blooded killer, and Walker needed him.

Fontane picked up Skip's six-gun and stuck it in his belt, then he and Trace lifted the body. As they carried the dead man out of the room and the house, Walker sat back on the edge of the desk, still trembling.

Eleanor came to his side, touching his arm. "It wasn't your fault, Sedge."

"No, it wasn't."

"Was it worth it?"

He looked at her pretty face and form, and he slid his arm around her, kissing her. "Yes."

"What about Maggie McBride?"

"She's a pretty woman, all right, but nothing like you. Besides, all I wanted was her gold. Fontane told me it had to be on their place. Trouble is, nothing's shown up since McBride was killed, so maybe she don't know where the rest of it is. Maybe no one does. Besides, there are other ways to get that land."

"So what do we do now?"

"You'll stay at the boarding house in McBride for three months. Then we'll marry. By that time, I'll be rid of Tanner."

"The bounty hunter?"

"Yes."

"Is he after you, Sedge?"

"I didn't say that."

"Are you afraid of him?"

"Maybe."

"Are you wanted?"

"Every man out here is wanted somewhere."

SEVEN

At Skip's funeral at the little cemetery outside of town, the sun was shining as the slight, graying preacher spoke of what a fine young man he was. Walker stood by with head bowed, hat in hand. Eleanor was in black with a veil and looking tearful. Most everyone from Walkersville attended.

Standing some fifty feet from the crowd with Harriman, Will, no longer wearing his sling, rubbed his chin in thought. "I wonder what really happened."

"You think he shot his own nephew?"

"Maybe."

"Over her?"

"Could be."

"You're cynical, Tanner."

"No. Just plumb wore out."

"Too wore out to dance?"

"What are you talking about?"

"The spring dance. A week from Saturday. At the McBride town hall."

"I ain't no dancer."

"It's easy. You just walk around and skip now and then."

"I came here lookin' for Grissom, that's all."

"You found him?"

"No."

Harriman grinned. "Maybe you'll find 'im at the dance."

It was later that evening as the two men stood outside of the gambling hall that Packard appeared across the street, glaring at them in the twilight. It was obvious trouble was coming. Packard had to regain his reputation.

"He's bound to try it," Harriman said.

"I got no proof he rode with Grissom."

"He could be wanted for somethin' else. Big reward, maybe."

"Stop needlin' me, Harriman. I ran bounties to have money to keep me on the trail. That's all."

They stood quiet as Packard came slowly into the street. There was no sign of Prudo, and there were no other men in sight, most having retired to toast Skip Walker, except for Pike. The sheriff was standing in the doorway of the express office, thumbs hooked in his gun belt.

"It's a setup," Harriman said.

"Then cover my back."

Packard suddenly shouted. "You, Tanner. I'm sick of lookin' at you."

"I'm not fightin' you, Packard."

"Yellow, Tanner?"

"Maybe."

"I'm goin' to kill you whether you pull that gun or not. And the sheriff there, he's gonna make it out to be a fair fight. So if I was you, I'd do somethin' about it."

"He's right," Harriman muttered.

Will slowly stepped into the street. Sweat was trickling down his rear. He figured Packard was just mad over the fight, and he had no stomach for killing him. But it was plenty obvious Packard was going to draw whether Will did or not.

Facing each other in the twilight, the two men surveyed the twenty feet between them. Packard was smiling, his mouth crooked, sweat on his thin nose, hat pushed back from his blond hair. He was polished and shiny, long fingers dangling near his six-gun.

Will felt shivers running down his back, not knowing where the bullets would come from. No one liked a bounty hunter. From the corner of his eye, he saw Harriman watching, and he prayed the detective would spot any back shooter.

Packard snickered. "I can see that yellow streak from here, Tanner."

"Do what you have to do, Packard."

Packard grinned, but his eyes narrowed, and suddenly his sneer was tightened. His head came down some, and his right arm hunched. He drew fast and sure.

But before he could pull the trigger, Will Tanner's six-gun was in his hand. Both men fired at the same time, shots echoing the street.

Other shots rang out from a window above the express office, but the shots went wild as Harriman fired, and a scrubby man came hurtling out the window and bounced off the roof of the office, then crashed crazily into the street.

Will stood with feet apart, six-gun hot in his hand, his heart pounding. And Packard dropped to his knees, blood on his shirt, but he fired at Will, the bullet whistling by Will's neck, and Will leaped aside, firing again.

Packard had two bullets in his chest, but he raised his gun to fire once more, then swayed and fell face down and kicked twice before dying in the mud.

Slowly, Will turned to look at Pike, who had come outside.

"You got somethin' to say?" Will demanded.

Harriman came forward and spoke up. "It was a fair fight, sheriff. And that man over there tried to make it otherwise."

Pike looked from the dead Packard to the dead back shooter, and he was grim but silent. Harriman came out into the street where Will was still standing with six-gun in hand.

"Come on, Tanner."

Will's throat was dry and burning. He was drenched with sweat. He saw that men had come into the street to look things over, and he glanced at the silent Pike. In front of the gambling hall, he saw the crazy-eyed Domino with a big cigar in his mouth, snickering.

Will shrugged and allowed Harriman to take him over to the cafe where he downed some hot coffee and tried to control himself. He found his hands were shaking, and his knees were weak. There were other men at the tables on the other side of the cafe, and he tried to compose himself.

"Big bad bounty hunter," Harriman said softly. "You're a wreck."

Will sipped more of the coffee, but he didn't answer.

"Listen, Tanner, all you're doin' is hanging out your sign for Grissom and his men to come and get you. But you're known as a bounty hunter, so every man in this town who's wanted, and I'll wager there are plenty of them, is goin' to haul down on you. You saw how Domino looks at you? And Pike? And you still got Prudo out there. And a few others. You can't stay alive forever."

"So what do you suggest?"

"Get out of town for a while."

"Such as?"

Harriman grinned. "I got a hankerin' for Maggie McBride's peach pie."

"You got an excuse to go out there?"

"We'll say we're on our way to Grady's and just stopped by."

"We ain't gonna find Grissom that way."

"No, maybe not. But someone killed McBride to get his gold mine. You know anyone greedier than Grissom?"

"But goin' to the ranch won't give us any answers."

Harriman leaned back. "From my experience, folks know more than they realize. You just got to talk it out of 'em."

"Then you go on ahead. I'll see if Timothy's got anything he forgot."

"Are you afraid of Darcie McBride?"

"Yeah, maybe I am. So what?"

As much as Will protested, he found himself packed up the next morning and riding with Harriman, west along the river. It was a morning with darkening clouds, and the cold was cutting through their britches. They huddled in leather jackets.

In the early afternoon, they saw a man lying on his belly along Tonto Creek. A young man with reddish hair, blood on his upper back, legs sprawled, no horse in sight.

"My God," Will breathed. "It's Ricky."

While Harriman stood watch with his Winchester drawn, Will jumped down and ran over to the prone figure, turning him over, holding his hand over the bloody chest.

"He's alive. Let's get him to the ranch, pronto."

The two men loaded Ricky onto Harriman's horse, and

Harriman sat with the youth in his arms, but Will was reading signs.

"More tracks comin' across the creek. I'll bet Darcie was out here with him. You go on ahead."

Harriman turned and took off at a lope.

It was already drizzling, but Will saw where a single horse had jumped to the east and taken off over the hills. Darcie, following the killers.

Sweat all over, Will got back in the saddle and headed after the prints at a trot and then a lope. The roll of the hills hid the next drop in the land, and anywhere he rode, a bullet could be waiting.

Then he saw Darcie's roan standing near some aspen.

He reined up, looked around as he drew his Winchester repeater, then slowly moved forward. There were other prints here. One horse with a thrown shoe. She had crossed its trail, and it looked like the man had ambushed her.

And then he spotted her down in a ditch, lying on her back.

Will was frantic. He dismounted and slid down the slope to her side. Blood was on the side of her head where a bullet had grazed her, but she was alive. He had read the signs easy enough. Whoever had shot her had come back, stopped, looked down without dismounting, and then had kept going, figuring she was dead.

He tied his bandanna around her head, then knelt to lift her in his arms. To his delight, she opened her eyes and gazed at him, lashes flickering as she moaned, her voice barely audible.

"Ricky's dead. He shot Ricky."

"No, he's alive."

She tried to speak, then fainted. She felt terribly small and fragile as he carried her up to his horse, setting her in the saddle, then putting his slicker around her before mounting behind her, holding her against him. He turned, heading back with her horse trailing.

Now it was raining heavy, wiping out the signs. He tried to keep the slicker about her while he huddled in his coat. Rain dribbled off his hat. She was semiconscious, clinging to him and moaning now and then.

Will silently prayed that she and her brother would' live.

When he reached the ranch house, Harriman and Maggie came running outside in the rain, and he lowered Darcie into Harriman's arms. Maggie was in tears, and Toby was watching from the doorway.

Will was so shaken, he turned and rode for the corral to put the horses away. Ricky's horse was standing outside the corral, and Will unsaddled it as well. Wearing his slicker, Toby came down from the house as Will was putting the horses in the enclosure, and the boy spoke angrily as rain poured off them.

"I know it was that Walker. He sent his men to do this. He wants this ranch. Mom wouldn't marry 'im, so he's trying to scare us off, that's what."

"You can't prove that, son." And Will's mouth went dry with the word.

"He ain't never gonna find that gold mine 'cause I ain't gonna tell 'im where it is." As soon as Toby ' spoke, he caught his breath and put his hand over his mouth.

"It's all right, son. I don't want your gold mine. But how is it you're the only one who's found it?"

"I didn't. I followed Pa once."

"Why didn't you tell your mother?"

"I was scared if we started showin' any more gold, they'd kill us for it. And I figured I should wait until we was real desperate."

Will was thoughtful as he studied him. "That's a lot for a boy to carry around."

"You won't tell nobody, will you?"

"No."

Toby grinned. "I knew I could trust you, Will. There's somethin' about you I like."

Will swallowed hard. He turned and put the saddle on the fence, then put the horses into the corral and gave them some grain. He turned again to see Toby's worried face.

"Come on, Will. I want to see how Darcie is."

"What about Ricky?"

"He's okay. Mom says he'll live. She got the bullet out already."

"What?"

"Mom took the bullet out. Come on."

Awed, Will followed the boy up the path as night fell, and they went into the house where a fire was blazing in the hearth and Darcie lay in front of it, covered with blankets. Will's red bandanna had been washed and was hanging on a rod in front of the mantel.

Harriman was standing by the table where Ricky lay covered with blankets and mumbling.

Maggie was boiling more water on the iron stove, but she turned to Will with a relieved smile. "He'll be all right."

But Will was more worried about Darcie and went to kneel at her side.

EIGHT

Kneeling by Darcie, the firelight dancing in her hair, Will was relieved to see her blue eyes fixed on him. She had a bandage around her head and was smiling. He reached down to draw the blanket up around her chin. His hand rested just a moment near her face, aching to touch her, but he sat back on his heels.

"Mom says you found me."

"What happened out there?"

"Ricky and me, we were riding along the creek looking for strays. Someone started shooting at us. Ricky rode in front of me and chased me into the trees. He took the bullet trying to cover me. He saved my life. And I thought for sure he was dead."

"Did you see who done it?"

"He was too far away when I saw him, but I followed. He was on a sorrel. He could have been anyone in a heavy wool coat. Then he bushwhacked me."

"You shouldn't have done it. That was a man's job."

She gazed up at him a long moment, about to argue, but then she smiled. "Maybe you're right."

He put his hand on her brow. She was feverish. Will stood up, looking worried, but Maggie held up her hand.

"She'll be all right. Now if you and Mr. Harriman will carry Ricky into his room, we'll cover him well. Toby can keep an eye on him while I feed the two of you."

And so later, with Ricky sleeping peacefully in his bed and Toby at his side, Will and Harriman sat at the table while Maggie fed them. Darcie still lay in front of the fire, and Maggie took her broth but no more. Soon, Darcie had her eyes closed.

Maggie was angry. "If I knew where that gold was, I'd give it to them."

"Well," Harriman said, "I think I'd better stick around awhile if you can put up with me."

"We always have room for you, Mr. Harriman. And Mr. Tanner, if he likes."

"Then I think I'll tum in," Harriman said. "After a meal like this, all I want to do is sleep."

Maggie's eyes were glistening as she smiled at him, and Harriman went to Ricky's room where Toby was waiting. Darcie turned in her blankets and gazed at her mother and Will.

"Darcie," Maggie said, "you should be asleep."

"I want Will to sing to me first."

Will lost his color and stared at her as he tied his bandanna back around his neck. Sing? The last time he had done that was eight years ago. But she pleaded, and he took down the guitar to sit near her, gazing into the fire as he tickled the strings. His voice was casual and deep.

Darcie's eyes closed as he sang of the changes in Texas, of the old cowhand who hated barbed wire and homesteaders who had "plowed and fenced" his cattle range. And how he was heading north.

He sang on with the verses, but once he figured Darcie was sleeping, Will found himself playing "The Yellow Rose of Texas" and singing more softly.

When he finished playing, he sat a long moment, staring into the fire, remembering, and wondering if he could ever love again, because if he could, it would be Darcie McBride.

As he stood to hang up the guitar, he suddenly remembered Maggie was there. A little embarrassed about singing a love song, he turned to see her pouring him another cup of hot coffee at the table.

"Sit down, Mr. Tanner."

He obeyed like a child as she leaned back in her chair and looked at Darcie where she lay sleeping.

Maggie spoke softly. "I have to thank you, Mr. Tanner. She might have died out there in the rain and cold."

"I'm glad she's all right. And it seems like you're better than any doctor."

"I learned the hard way, Mr. Tanner. In the war, I took bullets and pieces of metal out of men from both sides and even sewed them up. And when they lost a leg or arm, I held them as they cried. Near broke my heart. When I joined my husband out here, I thought it was all behind me, but this was not an open country. He was shot many times. And picked up an arrow or two."

"But still you managed to have Toby."

She glanced at him. "Yes."

"Toby has dark brown, almost black hair. And brown eyes. And high cheekbones."

69

"Like my grandfather."

Will shrugged. "You're lucky to have him."

He sipped his coffee, knowing she was watching him. After a moment, she spoke warily.

"My daughter thinks you're some kind of hero, Mr. Tanner."

Will was uneasy under her gaze, and he sipped the fresh hot coffee. "I have nothing but respect for your daughter. But as soon as I finish what I come for, I'm ridin' off."

"Like a wounded animal, looking for a place to die?"

Will's face was hot. Sweat was in his hair and all over his body. Maggie's penetrating gaze was too much. It was as if she was looking through his dark eyes into his very soul, and he had never felt so vulnerable. Nor had she ever been more right.

She leaned toward him. "We both know you're not the man in that dime novel. You ain't no different than any other man who's full of hurt. I can see it burning in your eyes, all the time. Who do you hate, Mr. Tanner?"

Will hesitated, but this woman had seen him kissing her daughter as if he could never stop, and she deserved some kind of explanation, something he had never felt he had to tell anyone else. He glanced at Darcie, her eyes closed and breathing gently. He gazed at the crackling fire, hearing the rain steady on the board roof as he answered.

"Hank Grissom and his men."

"The outlaw in the story?"

"He was real enough."

"And why do you hate him?"

"He killed my wife and son."

Maggie drew back in surprise, her face slowly losing its color. "I'm so sorry."

"His trail leads to this valley."

She placed her hands around her warm cup as she stared at the curling steam. "So all these men you killed, it was because of Grissom."

"Yes."

"How old was your son?"

"Six weeks," he said as his eyes brimmed. And as he told about the express office robbery and the grave, he tried to choke back his tears. Telling how he had wanted to dig up the mound to find the locket, but could not bring himself to do it; it was too much, and his tears came trickling down his rough face. He couldn't stop until he had said it all. He felt drained as he wiped his face with his bandanna.

"I'm sorry," she whispered, her own tears on her cheeks.

"A few years ago, I lost their trail. Now I've picked it up again. There's Grissom and four others left. And I ain't gonna rest until the job is done."

Will felt burning in his throat and chest. He was sweating all over, but he had never felt better, as if a poison had been leeched from him.

"How long ago was this?"

"Eight years last January."

She gazed at him through her tears and was choking on her words. "Thank you for telling me."

"It was a long time ago."

"Not for you," she said, gently.

Will got up clumsily, and he nodded his thanks, then turned to go to Ricky's room for the night. He paused to stare at Toby in the doorway, the boy sniffing back his own tears and twisting his fingers in his nightshirt. Will went to his side and put his

71

hand on the boy's shoulder, and they went into the room together.

Maggie stared after them as the door closed behind them, her own tears flowing freely as her heart ached. She turned to see Darcie's head roll toward her, and she saw tears trickling down her daughter's face. Neither spoke. There was no need.

The next morning, Ricky was in pain but awake and doing well with no fever. Toby stayed with him while Harriman and Will enjoyed a hearty breakfast, Darcie joining them, her head still bandaged. She looked wonderful, but she was not in a good mood and appeared weak as she sat back in her chair.

"Now what?" she asked. "Do we just sit here and let them pick us off one by one?"

Maggie frowned. "I suppose there's no use goin' to Pike. We need to get the U.S. Marshal here. I'll ask Mr. Grady to send a message with the stage driver. No one would suspect him."

"Never mind," Harriman said. "I'll take care of it."

"First thing," Will said, "I'm going to see Walker."

Maggie looked at him strangely. "Is that wise?"

"There's some suspicion he had your husband killed. And now he must be figurin' that Darcie and Ricky are stopping the wedding."

Maggie flushed. "I never really said no. Just said I'd think about it. He is a very fine man."

"He got tired of waitin'."

"You're making a lot of assumptions, Mr. Tanner." Harriman cleared his throat. "Well, uh, Maggie, I hate to tell you this, but I agree with Tanner. Walker's got the scent of gold, and he ain't givin' up."

"But Mr. Walker's a gentleman. A lawyer."

"He has money," Harriman said. "He can pay others to do his dirty work."

Will nodded. "The man who shot Ricky and Darcie headed south toward Walker's, not town. And I'm about to find out if Trace's horse has a new shoe on its right front hoof."

"I'm goin' with you," Harriman said. "You'll need a witness in that hornets' nest."

"I don't like these folks bein' alone," Will said.

Maggie straightened. "Don't you worry about us, Mr. Tanner. Darcie and I can shoot as good as any man."

"Stay close to home then."

He stood up, pulled on his leather coat and donned his worn Stetson. Then he took up his Winchester, bedroll, and saddlebags from Ricky's room, pausing' to gaze at the ailing youth, who was grinning at him.

"I heard you singin' last night, Will. You sound like a frog."

Will grinned back at him. "So I do."

"How's Darcie?"

"She's all right, thanks to you. Takes a full grown man to risk his life to save another."

Ricky lay back, grateful for the words.

Toby stood up and grabbed Will's sleeve. "We heard what you was gonna do. But you gotta be careful. That Trace is a real bad man."

Will paused, gazing down at the boy. "I know." Then he went back into the front room.

Harriman was still sipping his coffee. "I'll be along in a minute, Tanner."

Leaving the house, Will felt as if he was leaving home. Ricky could have been his brother, and Toby was like the son he had lost, looking enough like Will to make a man wonder. Maggie was like the mother he had never known. And Darcie, she was...

"Will."

He paused on the trail and turned to see Darcie coming down the path in the cold morning air, a blanket wrapped around her. Sunlight danced on her red hair and freckles, and she looked pale but lovely, even with the bandage about her forehead.

She stopped a few feet from him, a tear trickling down her left cheek. "I heard what you told Mom last night. You're no bounty hunter, Will Tanner. You're just a man who was hurt real bad. And I don't believe you ever killed anyone unless you had to."

He pulled his hat down tight. "Good-bye, Darcie."

He turned away, but he heard her running after him, and she caught his arm, turning him around forcefully. Her blue eyes were dark and gleaming, her chin up, soft hair falling about her pretty face.

"Don't you ever say good-bye to me, Will Tanner."

She slid her hand up to his neck and pulled his head down, then pressed her soft lips to his rough ones, sending waves of shock through him. When she released him, he staggered back a step, his face hot.

"It's no use, Darcie. I'm no good for anyone."

He paused to stare at her, and then he turned away. He told himself nothing could bring him back. But she had come awful close with that kiss. In fact, he was shaking all over.

He went down to the corrals and started saddling his black. Harriman came down to join him, and soon they were riding south over the rolling hills. It was cold and windy, and the sky was cloudy in the north.

"That Maggie is really getting to me," Harriman said. "Now I see what I've been missin'."

"You think she'd have an old varmint like you?"

"I'd like to find out."

"Then why are you takin' chances? Go on back."

"I ain't lettin' you get killed, Tanner. If I did, I'd never find Grissom."

"That's real touching."

Will had to grin, and they were in sight of the Walker mansion by late afternoon. They rode through herds of cattle, longhorns and white face, and a lot of horses.

The corrals and outbuildings were in good repair, and there was a mare and colt in one of the enclosures. In another, a sorrel horse was standing alone. There were no men around, despite the large bunkhouse near which they reined to a halt, out of sight of the house.

Will dismounted and walked into the corral where the sorrel lifted its head to watch him. "Whoa, boy."

Will put his hand on the animal's neck and soothed it, running his fingers down to the right foreleg. Sure enough, it was missing a shoe. He left the corral and mounted again, nodding to Harriman as they rode around the bunkhouse, then reined to a halt.

Up at the mansion with its circling porch and balcony, they could see a black horse and buggy loaded with luggage. And there was Skip Walker's fiance standing on the porch with her back to them. Walker came outside in a long black coat and grabbed her in a hungry embrace, and they were kissing.

"Now ain't that interesting," Harriman said.

"Then why is she leaving?"

"Propriety."

Will frowned, and both men were wondering what had really happened to Skip Walker.

Riding up the hill, they saw Walker turn with the woman, and the pair came to an abrupt halt on the steps, both staring at the oncoming intruders.

As the riders reined up by the buggy, Walker glared at them with red face, his heavy brows low over his pale eyes.

"What do you want here?"

Will was grim. "Someone tried to murder Ricky and Darcie McBride yesterday."

"Sorry to hear that, but why are you here?"

"That sorrel in the corral. Who belongs to it?"

"Every man on this spread has five or six horses in his string. It could be anyone's."

Eleanor had recovered and was smiling, her hand on Walker's arm. "Why, Sedge, don't you remember? That was Trace's horse."

Walker was frowning, but as he gazed at her, he suddenly smiled. "Why, I do believe you're right."

"Where will I find Trace?"

"He's gone to town on business."

Will looked from Walker to the woman, and his mouth went tight, then he turned his horse about.

Walker drew a deep breath as the men rode down the hillside and past the corrals. "You know, Eleanor, we're going to get along just fine. You've just set Tanner up."

"So was it Trace's horse?"

"Sure was."

"So what happens now?"

"Tanner will be tangling with Trace."

"Will Trace win?"

"You can bet on it."

NINE

As they rode toward town, Will glanced back toward the Walker spread more than once. "A man who would shoot his own nephew could be anyone."

"Walker's an educated man. Nobody like that was riding with those killers. Now you find the real Grissom, he'll be someone like Pike, or Domino, or Trace, or even Fontane."

"Maybe, but Trace didn't go after the McBrides without being paid for it."

It was nightfall when they rode into Walkersville. They reined up in front of the sheriff's office. Pike came to stand in the doorway, the lamplight framing his huge body.

"What do you want, Tanner?"

"Someone shot Ricky and Darcie McBride."

"Well, I got no jurisdiction out there."

"You seen Trace?"

"Over at the Golden Wheel."

The two riders turned their mounts and rode over to the gambling hall where several horses were at the railing, then turned and rode to the front of the cafe. Here they dismounted and tied their horses. Surveying the town, they could see lights in many buildings, including the express office, and a lot of horses in front of the saloons and miner's hotel. But there were no men on the streets. The town was very quiet.

"I'll go around the back," Harriman said. "Give me a few minutes."

Will nodded and walked slowly down the boardwalk from the cafe, past a smoke-filled saloon and toward the gambling hall. He could feel sweat trickling down his back and rear. His face was damp. His upper back where he had been shot was still feeling the chill of night. His right hand dangled at his side near his holster.

Trace was not a man who had to brag about his skill with a gun, that was obvious, but it was just as clear he would have no hesitation about ambushing the McBrides. Everything about the man had defined him as evil. And therefore the question was, was Trace actually Grissom or one of his men?

And what about Domino? He could see him through the dirty windows, standing over by the roulette wheel, his arms folded, a big cigar in his mouth. Will paused, looking at the man with his short black beard, the diamond studs gleaming in the lamplight, his black hair slicked back.

Will couldn't see Trace until he got to the swinging doors. Standing at the far end of the bar on the right, the man was drinking whiskey and talking to the bartender. The conchos on his hat band were gleaming, and his wool coat was on the bar. He was wearing a grey, double-breasted shirt.

A dozen other men were playing poker. Two who looked like miners were at the wheel. Three were at the bar with Trace.

Now Trace was turning to follow the bartender's gaze, and

his thin black mustache twisted as he smiled, his black eyes like hot little coals.

"Well now."

Will entered and moved aside to keep his back to the wall. He stood quiet, surveying the room, wondering if there really was a back door for Harriman to find.

The poker players fell silent, looked from Trace to Will, grabbed their money and scrambled from their chairs, then hurried over near the roulette wheel where Domino was still smiling. The three men at the bar suddenly moved aside, over toward the wheel on the left.

Trace remained, and the bartender slowly walked to the left as well, but he had something out of sight, in his hands. Likely a shotgun. There appeared to be a back door behind where the gunman was standing. "Mr. Tanner," said Trace, straightening as he set his whiskey glass aside. "Are you looking for me?"

"Your sorrel threw a shoe. Over on McBride's place."

"So it did."

"You took shots at a boy and a woman."

"Did I?"

"They're alive, Trace. And they can identify you."

Trace continued to smile, but his eyes were searing. "No one's going to believe them, Tanner. So you're wasting your time."

Will's lips spread tight, his legs like stone. He wondered if he could move fast if he had to. He watched the way Trace was slowly positioning himself with feet apart.

"There's no law around here," Will said. "I'm takin' you down to Pueblo."

"You sound like a bounty hunter, my friend."

"I came here lookin' for Grissom. Maybe that's who you really are."

"Wrong again."

Trace shuffled his shoulders as he shifted his weight a little. He showed confidence and a lot of experience as he smiled easily.

"Tanner, if you don't leave, you're going to die right where you stand."

"I'm not leaving."

Trace shifted his hips a little, his hands at his side. "Why do you wear two guns? Showin' off?"

"You ain't talkin' your way out of this one. I'm taking you to Pueblo."

"I've killed seven men, Tanner. You're going to be number eight."

"You get 'em in the back?"

Trace snickered. "I've seen you draw. I can beat sou right easy."

"Drop your belt or make your move."

Trace's dark eyes became slits in his face. Now!

His right hand swept up his six-gun, but Will drew faster, and before Trace could pull the trigger, Will was firing. A bullet hit Trace in the left shoulder, and Trace could have lived, but he yelled and lifted his sixgun, firing at Will, who darted aside and shot back, putting a bullet in Trace's thigh.

Trace dropped to his knees, and he fired again. This time, the bullet whistled by Will's ear. Will fired again to try to wound him, but Trace fell forward, and the bullet slammed into the man's chest instead of his leg.

Trace fell onto his stomach and tried to roll over, but before he could fire again, Will was there with his boot on the man's gun arm at the wrist.

Trace stared up at him, his eyes glazing. "A priest. I need a priest."

"There's no priest here," Will said. "You'll have to confess to me. Did you kill my wife?"

Trace gasped. "The dancer in Laredo? I didn't mean to hurt her that bad."

"No, it was—"

"That school teacher in Houston?"

"No, the woman and child from Pecos Junction." Blood trickled from Trace's mouth. "Pecos Junction? That's all? That's why you were after us?"

"That's right."

"You're crazy. No one laid a hand on 'em. It was an accident. They fell from the cliff when some rocks gave way."

"Who buried 'em?"

Trace was choking on his own blood. "I didn't wait around to find out. We all scattered. Now get me a priest."

"Is Grissom in this valley?"

"Yes. For God's sake, get me a priest."

"Who is he?" Will demanded. "Who are the other three?"

The little preacher came hurrying inside and knelt, shoving Will's boot off the man's arm. "There, there, man, he can't hurt you now."

Then Trace held up the six-gun and fired, the bullet tearing into the flesh of Will's left arm above the elbow. Staggering back in fury, Will raised his six-gun despite the preacher's dirty look.

Trace dropped his weapon and clung to the preacher, who was shoving a cross in his hand. But it was too late. Trace closed his eyes forever. A killer of men and women, attempted killer of the McBrides, he would kill no more.

The preacher straightened. "You killed this man."

"In self-defense," Harriman said, standing behind the bar with his six-gun aimed at the bartender. "That man tried to murder Ricky and Darcie McBride. And he's killed a lot of men. And a woman in Laredo, it seems. And a school teacher."

The preacher turned sad. "I'm sorry. I didn't know."

Domino walked casually over and looked down at the dead man. "Too bad. He was a big gambler."

Will glared at him. "Yeah? Maybe he was about to name you, Domino. Maybe you're Grissom. How about it?"

"You're wounded, Tanner," Domino said with a sneer. "You're out of your head."

And with arrogance, Domino turned his back on Will.

Pike was standing in the doorway taking it all in, and he was making a face as mean as he could. "Tanner, you're nothing but trouble. I want you out of this town."

Will stood with his six-gun in his left hand, his right fingers gripping the bleeding wound on his left arm. Harriman came from around the bar with six-gun in hand and joined Will, both moving so no one was behind them.

"Pike," Harriman said, "you can just get out of our way."

"I'm the sheriff in this here town."

"You're not duly elected."

"I'm still sheriff."

"And I'm a Deputy U.S. Marshal."

Pike was staggered, and everyone stared.

Will turned in dismay. "Blast you, Harriman. You said you were a Wells Fargo Detective."

"I lied. We can do that, you know."

Harriman switched his six-gun to his left hand, then reached inside his vest and drew out a shining star, which he pinned to the leather. He tossed his six-gun back to his right grip and started toward the door with Will trailing.

Pike gritted his teeth and moved aside as the two men headed for the moonlight.

Out in the street, Will headed toward McBride where he knew Elmer would take care of him at the hotel. He kept glaring at Harriman.

"Why'd you lie to me?"

"Wanted to know more about you."

"Is your name Harriman?"

"Yep."

"Well, that's somethin'."

"You know when a man gets mad, his blood races, and he bleeds more, so if I were you, Tanner, I'd calm down."

Will stomped over the bridge with Harriman at his heels, and they headed for the hotel. "Listen to me, Harriman. That star ain't gonna help you none. You just made yourself a target. Why didn't you wait?"

"Pike needed settin' back."

"Yeah, well, now we're both targets. You might as well stick your head between your legs and kiss your behind good-bye, because they'll be comin' after you."

They climbed the steps of the hotel with Will bleeding all over the place and the desk clerk fussing over the mess. Elmer came down to fix Will's arm, while Timothy had to know everything that had happened.

"Well, now we're gettin' some place," Timothy said, tugging at his beard. "Federal law in town. Now that's some thin'."

Elmer patted the sling. "By golly, you keep this up, I'll hang up my shingle."

Later in the cafe, Harriman and Will had supper, and the lawman grinned at his weary companion. "You know, Will, you ought to give up this kind of life. It's wearing you out."

"You' re right about that."

"Now if'n you'd marry Darcie, I'd be your stepfather."

"I'm not fit for any woman, not anymore."

"So you think you died eight years ago."

"That's about it."

"I saw Darcie kiss you on the trail from the house. You jumped six feet. You looked alive to me."

"I ain't gettin' married, and that's it. A man can only go through that once. When my wife and son died, I went right along with 'em."

"All right, simmer down. You're worse'n a green colt."

"And you keep needlin' me."

"Didn't know you could needle a dead man."

"You keep this up, Harriman, and you'll be real dead."

Harriman grinned. "Take it easy."

"Now are we here to get Grissom or not?"

"We?"

"There you go again," Will growled.

"Yes, you're right," Harriman said, chuckling. "I just can't help it. It's kind of like teasin' a turkey buzzard. They don't fly off if they' re real hungry. They just snap at you."

"All right, so I'm hungry for Grissom."

Harriman leaned back with his coffee cup in his hand and he sobered. "Well, I guess you're back to normal. So here's the thing. You've got Trace. That leaves Grissom and three others. We've both cased this town and everyone in it. I've been up to the mines. It still comes down to some of the hardcases around here, including Pike, Fontane, or Domino."

"I vote for Walker. He's civilized enough to have gone back and buried my wife and son."

Harriman shrugged. "I still don't believe Walker's our man. Grissom was a cold-blooded killer. Men who'd ride with him would have to be the same."

"Maybe, but they started out as soldiers, remember?"

"At least you know what happened to your family was an accident."

"I figured it was, but I'm sure of it now."

"Well, we ain't gettin' nothin' done sittin' here. I figure we'd better get out to the McBrides' and make sure no one's pullin' anything else out there."

"You go ahead. I'm going to keep an eye on Domino and Pike."

"Not a chance. You're goin' with me so I can keep an eye on you, Tanner."

"What?"

"I want you with me."

"You arrestin' me for somethin'?"

"Yeah, for havin' a fat head. Are you comin' or not?"

Will grumbled to himself, but he was soon riding into the night with the grinning Harriman. It was raining again, and they pulled their slickers, riding with their heads bent and water pouring off their hats.

TEN

At the McBride's later that night, Darcie and Toby were out at the barn, trying to secure a broken door. The horses were inside, nickering and pacing about as lightning flashed and thunder rolled, rumbling across the sky like a dozen locomotives.

Up at the house, Ricky was able to sit up by the fire, but he was nervous as the house shook in the rain. Thunder made the roof shudder. Maggie was busy with the stew.

"Mr. Harriman was sure smitten with you, Mom."

"Don't be silly. He's practically a stranger."

"I like 'im."

"You do?" she asked, brightening. "But what about Mr. Walker and all his money?"

"And Grady and all his peaches?"

She laughed. "Yes, all right. Maybe I would rather have the peaches. But you know, one bad winter, and he wouldn't have any."

"And Walker could lose all his money."

"So what does Mr. Harriman have to lose?"

"He said he never loses," Ricky said with a grin, but then he sobered. "Nah, you don't want no professional gambler, Mom. When they get to losin', everything goes. The ranch, you, whatever he's got to bet with."

"Why, Ricky, where do you learn all this? Have you been hanging around that gambling hall?"

"No, Mom, honest."

She tried to peer out the window. "They are taking an awful long time."

"Did you see how Darcie was taken with that Tanner?"

She frowned. "Yes, I know."

"And Toby, he just about worships him. By the way, Mom, did you notice how much Toby looks like ole Will?"

"What are you saying?"

"Toby could be Will's brother by the looks of 'em together."

"Ricky, that's foolish talk. Don't be putting any silly ideas in Toby's head. Do you want him riding off with a bounty hunter?"

Maggie went about working the dough for biscuits, kneading it with a fury.

Suddenly, the door burst open, and Toby came charging in with Darcie on his heels, and rain and wind followed them. The two turned quickly and fought valiantly to close the door, finally succeeding and putting the bar in place.

Darcie was laughing as she pulled off her slicker and hurried to the fire. "It's freezing out there."

"Darcie wanted to get up on the roof," Toby said, "but I wouldn't let her."

"It was leaking all over the hay we cut," Darcie complained. "And I couldn't fix the door either. All that work cutting hay, and sometime this summer, it's gonna smolder and burst into flame, you watch."

Maggie shrugged. "I've never seen that happen, so maybe it's just a story."

Toby hung up his slicker and came to the fire to warm his hands. They were both shivering, and Ricky teased them. Maggie put the biscuits in the dutch oven and glanced at her children, loving everyone of them, but terrified they would be shot; murdered, all for the gold. Everyone could be after it, Walker, the gunmen in town, Harriman, and even Will Tanner.

Later in the night, when Maggie was serving stew, a pounding on the door frightened her. Ricky reached for the Winchester near his chair. Darcie grabbed one off the rack, and Toby took up an old Army Colt.

Maggie glanced out the window, but she could see nothing in the dark rain. Wiping her hands on her apron, she moved slowly toward the door. "Who is it?" she called.

"Your knight in shining armor," Harriman shouted.

Hurriedly, Maggie drew the bar across the slots and dropped it. Harriman came rushing in with Will on his heels and another flood of rain. The two men quickly turned and barred the door.

Rain dripping from his slicker, Harriman was grinning and puffing. "Whew. Boy, does something smell good."

Will was afraid to look toward Darcie, so he busied himself taking off his slicker, Toby suddenly there to help tug at the sleeves.

Harriman was still talking. "We'd have been in sooner, but we had to nail some boards on the .roof. And we reset that barn door for you. You know, if you ain't careful, when hay gets wet like that, it can smolder and—"

"Catch on fire," Maggie said, smiling. "Now go wash your hands. There's plenty of stew and biscuits."

"You knew we were coming?" Harriman asked as he hung up his slicker. When he turned, the star on his vest was shining in the lamp and firelight. Everyone was staring. "Oh, this old thing."

Toby hurried over. "Wow. Deputy United States Marshal. Where'd you get it?"

"In a poker game," Harriman said, grinning.

"Really?"

"Nah, I've had it all along. Me and Will, we've been doin' a job together."

"Really?"

Will looked at the boy's wide eyes, and he was grateful to Harriman for giving Will some respectability after all. He glanced toward Darcie and her mother as they hurriedly set out more food and plates, and it was obvious that Maggie was thoroughly impressed, her cheeks a bright rose.

"Yeah," Harriman said, wiping his face with a towel, "we're going to get Grissom sooner or later."

"What happened at Walker's?" Ricky asked.

"Well," the lawman said, "it was somethin' all right. We rode over there and saw that Miss Eleanor huggin' and kissin' ole Walker."

Maggie turned, stunned. "What does it mean?"

"Well, it makes you wonder why ole Skip died."

Toby was excited. "You think she killed Skip to get the ranch and Mr. Walker?"

Harriman chuckled. "Now, I never thought of it that way. Anyhow, it was Trace's horse all right, missing one shoe. So Tanner and me, we headed to town, lookin' for 'im."

"And what happened?" Toby asked, breathless.

They sat at the table with Will and Harriman at either end. Maggie and Darcie sat on one side, with Darcie next to Will. Toby and a barely moving Ricky sat across from them, the boy next to Will.

As Maggie passed the stew, Herriman spoke softly, watching Toby's eyes get bigger. "We goes to the Golden Wheel, see, and I sneak around the back. Then Tanner here, he walks in the front like he owns the place. And ole Trace is waitin'."

As Harriman continued with his story, he dressed it up so much that Will was embarrassed. Why, even the preacher's appearance took on great emphasis. When he finished, everyone was staring in disbelief.

"Wow," Toby said, turning to Will. "Was you scared?"

Will hesitated. He hadn't been afraid for eight years. Yet the boy's shining brown eyes were so filled with wonder, he had to put some reason to it.

"Sure I was scared."

"He was afraid," Harriman said, "but he didn't quit. He faced that killer right down."

Maggie frowned. "Did Trace say who sent him?"

"No, but he works for Walker," the lawman said.

As they finally settled down to the meal, Maggie spoke. "I've been thinking. We haven't found the gold mine, and that's all Mr. Walker seems to want. Now he has some good meadowland in the south valley. Maybe he'd trade for our ranch and call off this war."

"Trade?" Darcie echoed.

"That'd be giving up," Ricky said.

Maggie looked uneasy. "Even if we sell the herd, it won't

be enough to pay what we owe. We're going to lose this place anyway."

Toby frowned and turned to Will. "What do you think, Will? Is it time?"

Will shrugged his big shoulders. "You got to think on it, Toby."

"Think on what?" Maggie asked.

But Toby's gaze was fixed on Will. "My Pa's buried here. We got to keep this place, no matter what happens."

Will nodded. "All right, then. That's it."

Toby gathered everyone in front of the fireplace, forcing Harriman and Will into the leather chairs. Ricky, Maggie, and Darcie settled down on the rug and pillows around the blazing fire. Everyone was curious.

"Now hear this," Toby said. "I'm going to save this ranch. I'm going to find the gold."

Ricky laughed. "You couldn't find your behind with both hands. What's got into you, anyhow?"

"Hush, Ricky," Darcie said. "Something's going on here."

Everyone waited as Toby held his audience in check. Then the boy spoke. "Me and Will, we agree it's time I done told you where the gold mine is."

"What?" Maggie gasped.

"That's right," Toby said. "I followed Pa's tracks one time. He didn't even see me, but I saw him go in this cave and how he hid the mine entrance with brush."

Darcie shook her head. "Playing Indian again."

"Be right glad I did," Toby said. "Pa never was in there for very long. He'd come out in a little while with that little tobacco sack he carried the gold in. Then he'd sit down and sleep awhile.

Make folks think he was gone a long ways off. I near froze watchin', but I knowed he'd tan my hide if he caught me. Come evenin', he just got up and covered the mine with brush. I had a heck of a time beatin' him back to the ranch."

Darcie was awe-stricken. "Gold. Everyone's going to come after it. They'll ruin the ranch."

"We'll be smart like Pa," Ricky said. "And take just enough to pay our bills as we go."

Toby made a face. "That is if I can still find it."

Ricky threw a punch at him from a distance, and Toby laughed. "Stop your funnin'," Ricky said.

Everyone fell silent again. Darcie got to her knees and hugged Toby. Maggie got up and went over to the stove, fiddling with the pans, rattling them. She was too shaken to hold anything in her hand.

Harriman got up and came to her side. "Maggie, are you all right?"

She turned with tears trickling down her face as she looked up at him. "Dear God, they'll kill us all."

He gripped her by the arms to hold her steady. "Not if I can help it."

She moved against him, touching his star, and he held her in his embrace while she sobbed. Darcie wept as she watched her mother.

"Women," Ricky said, trying to sit up straight. "Well, I ain't scared. We can all shoot. Even Toby."

"What do you mean, even Toby?" the boy snapped. "I won' that last match, didn't I?"

Darcie got to her knees again. "Will you two stop it? Mom's right. We're in a lot of trouble now. No matter what we do."

"As soon as the rain stops," Ricky said, "we're goin' up there."

Darcie stood up slowly and gazed at Will with awe. "Did you know this all along?"

Toby grinned. "Yeah, but he promised to keep it a secret."

Maggie, still comfortable in Harriman's strong arms, finally forced herself to draw back. She wiped her eyes with the edge of her apron and bashfully moved around him.

There was a quiet celebration at the McBrides' that night, but over at Walkersville, Walker had left Eleanor at the boarding house in McBride, promising her that a lot of gold would be hers, one way or another.

"I've never seen pure gold," she had said softly. "I'd like to run it through my fingers."

"I promise you'll have sacks of it."

Walker had smiled at her greed, for it complemented his own. He was going to find it if he had to kill every McBride, one by one, until someone talked.

But he had more on his mind than McBride's gold. Later on, in the middle of the night, he and three others conferred in the lamplight at the express office. Walker was sitting behind the desk, his fingertips together in deep thought.

Pike was pacing like a wounded grizzly. Domino sat in front of the desk with one knee crossing the other, his hat pushed back. And Fontane stood near the door, looking out at the rain.

"We can't do no thin' in this weather," Fontane said.

"We can't wait either," Pike countered. "A federal marshal starts nosin' around, he's gonna find out we been robbin' the U.S. Mail and takin' a pretty deep cut in all those gold shipments from the stamp mill. No tellin' what he's already found out."

"He'll find out a lot more," Fontane said. "We're all going to hang."

"But you kill a federal officer," Walker said, "you're going to have the army here. We got to do it right."

Pike moved his big hulk around. "I say let's bush-whack 'em both anyhow. Blame it on some miner lookin' for a grubstake."

"It's risky," Walker said.

Pike grunted. "You lawyers. What are you gonna do, paper him to death?"

"I'm not afraid to get it done," Walker snapped. "But let's not be stupid about it."

"Maybe," said Domino, "we could get them both in a way that makes it look like they had a shoot-out. Killed each other. Make sure someone like Grady finds 'em."

Walker smiled. "Yes. We'll get Switz. He'll do anything for a dollar."

ELEVEN

When the rain stopped the next morning, the McBrides prepared for their great discovery, but Maggie was reluctant to have Will and Harriman go with them.

"Mom," Toby said, "we got to trust 'em."

"Your mother's right," Harriman said.

When the four McBrides rode from the corral in the chill of early light, Harriman leaned on the fence and turned to Will. "We got to follow."

"What's on your mind?"

"Stolen gold from Gila City, Arizona Territory. So pure it didn't need processing. Gold earmarked for the Confederacy. Southern sympathizers had stolen it and were sending it to help fight the war. Grissom was the officer in charge of transporting it. This is as far as it got."

"Blast you, Harriman, what else haven't you told me?"

"McBride rode with Grissom."

Will pulled his hat down tight, his mouth twisted in a frown. "I sure hope you're wrong."

"Could be Maggie knows all about it. That's why she wasn't

too happy about goin' out to find it."

"She knew she was usin' stolen money?"

"Maybe."

"Great. Go ahead and arrest her. You oughta be good at that."

Harriman scowled. "Back off, Tanner. I ain't arrestin' no woman for tryin' to feed her family."

The two men saddled up and easily followed the trail in the mud. By late morning, they turned up a red rock canyon where they could see the McBrides' horses in a hollow. On the right were heaps of rocks at the bottom of the cliff wall. On the left, a high rise of rugged terrain, and ahead of the hollow, a grove of aspens.

On foot, Will and Harriman moved up through the rocks where they could see the family tearing the brush away from the cave entrance in a cliff wall. They were all in heavy coats, and Ricky was too weak to do anything but watch. Sunlight danced on them.

But when Toby came crawling out with a sack the size of a small melon, the boy was crying. Maggie sat back on a rock and put her face in her hands. Darcie stared at the stack, wiped her eyes and removed her hat. Ricky just shook his head. Toby shoved the sack away from him with a sob.

"Mom, this is stolen gold dust. Look, it says Gila City on it, and there are a whole bunch more sacks in there. Bigger ones. We got to give it to the marshal."

Maggie straightened. "Yes, we have to do that."

"Yeah," Ricky said, anxiously, "but where did Pa get it?"

Maggie wiped her brow. "It was gold on its way to help the South. But he never told me where it was hidden."

Darcie took up her Winchester. "We've got to tell the marshal right away."

Maggie nodded sadly. "Yes, and if we don't hurry, someone is surely going to kill us for it."

It was then that Harriman and Will came down from the rocks, and Darcie turned, Winchester leveled, uncertain what to do. But Maggie gazed tearfully at Harriman as she hugged herself in the chill.

"You knew all along, Mr. Harriman?"

"I just suspected. No pure gold up on the mountain. Not likely there'd be any down here either."

"There's a lot of sacks in there," Ricky said.

Harriman knelt and looked into the cave. "We'll leave a phony bag here and bury the rest near your house for safekeeping, except for one bag."

"One bag?" Ricky asked.

"Will and I are going to bait a trap."

Maggie smiled, wiping her eyes. "And you trust us to leave it alone?"

Harriman nodded, taking her hand to help her to her horse, and she leaned against him as his arm encircled her. They paused a moment by her horse, and she looked up at him with tears still on her face. With his free hand, he wiped them gently away.

Back at the ranch house that evening, sitting around the blazing fire with the one bag of gold on the table and the rest buried in a tarp in the barn, Maggie finally broke down and told them about McBride.

Her voice was wavering. "Captain Grissom and his men, including your father, were escorting the stolen gold into Colorado Territory on their way back to the war to help the

South, but the captain suddenly decided to hide it here in a cave. Your father and others protested, but Grissom was in charge.

"When they got back to Missouri, he soon had them raiding in civilian clothes, and before long, they were more outlaws than soldiers.

"Your father wanted out, but Grissom had killed others who had tried it. Then down in Texas at Pecos Junction, they robbed an express office, and Grissom took a woman and child as hostage. When they got to the Big Bend, her horse fell and took them both down to the river. Grissom was in a big hurry to get to Mexico, so your father was the only one who would stay to bury them."

As she caught her breath, she looked sadly at Will, whose face was drained of color, his dark eyes wet.

She looked at her unhappy children, then continued.

"Your father got up here before Grissom and hid the gold until he could turn it in. When Grissom and the others came and couldn't find it, they thought someone else had stumbled on it. Grissom never suspected your father or any of his men were brave enough to go against him."

Ricky looked sad. "But Pa started using the gold."

"Only because we were in danger of losing the ranch. That's when Grissom knew your father had it. And they must have beaten him, trying to make him talk, then shot him in anger. And they're still after it, and they'll do anything to get it. And we're going to lose the ranch anyway."

Will was on the edge of his chair. "So who are they? Who's Grissom?"

She shook her head. "I don't know who they are. My husband

kept us out of it so we wouldn't be hurt. He never told me anymore than what I just told you."

There was a long silence where only the sound of the crackling fire could be heard. Darcie and Maggie, sitting on the pillows, hugged each other. Toby was silent, poking at the fire with the iron.

Ricky drew his blanket more tightly around him as he settled down in his chair. "Is Walker one of the Grissom gang? Is he Grissom?"

Harriman and Will glanced at each other, and the lawman shrugged. "I think we're going to find out."

Toby looked up. "Can I set the trap?"

"No," Harriman said. "Will's going to 'find' the gold mine, and Will's going to be the bait. And the hero marshal will get 'em all."

Darcie looked strained. "But it's dangerous..."

"How you gonna do it?" Toby asked.

"Well, I suppose Will's just going to ride into town with this here gold and deposit it in Walker's express office. With Gila City on it, word's going to get out fast. And I figure it's Walker will take the bait."

Will glared at the lawman. "You suspected Walker all along."

"Yeah, well, sort of. But I like hearing you better like some longhorn cow lookin' for her calf, Tanner. You're real entertaining."

"You men stop it," Maggie said, her color fading. "I refused him because I thought he might be one of them. He bought off most of our place, but when I refused to sell the foothills, he got real suspicious and must have figured that's where the gold was. I saw some of his men riding the hills, and I know they were looking for it. And that's when he started asking me to marry him."

Maggie was still sitting on the pillow in front of the fire, and Darcie reached over to touch her hand. "It's all right, Mom. But you should have told us."

"I should have told you your father was an outlaw?"

"We all loved him just the same."

Maggie started to weep again, and Harriman, sitting on a wooden chair, bent forward to take her hand. He spoke gently.

"Maggie, it's all right. That was a lousy war for both sides. I was with the Union, and I can tell you this, nobody came out a winner. Your husband wasn't the only one who didn't surrender. And a lot more of 'em refused amnesty when it came out in '69. Some will never give up."

He released her hand, and she wiped her eyes. "I remember the amnesty," she said softly. "It was at Christmas."

No one spoke for a while, and then Darcie got up to set the table. Maggie drew herself together and went to help, and Ricky, exhausted, went to his room to lie down for a while.

But Toby, sitting on the rug in front of the fire, turned to look up at the two men who were in the leather chairs. He was serious, his voice apprehensive.

"So when you take the gold in, Will, does that mean you'll lead 'em back to the mine where the marshal will be waiting?"

"I reckon."

"But they'll all come, won't they?"

"Well, we figure Grissom and four others came to this valley. Trace was one of 'em. Your father must have been another. That leaves Grissom and two more. We ain't sure who they be, but we can handle 'em."

"Who does the gold belong to?" Toby asked.

Harriman crossed his left leg over his other knee. "Until it can be returned to the original owners, it'll be held by the federal government. And of course, you McBrides are going to get the reward."

Maggie looked up from the cooking pot. "Reward?"

"Sure. Five thousand."

They all stared at Harriman, and then Toby clapped his hands. "Whoopie! We won't lose the ranch, Mom. Ain't that wonderful? I got to tell Ricky."

Maggie turned away to hide her flood of tears.

But after everyone had turned in for the night, Harriman and Will sat alone in front of the crackling fire, and the lawman turned to him.

"After you got Trace, you got 'em all scared. They're liable to try any kind of ambush now."

"So they may be waitin' for us."

"You keep a good distance ahead of me. I'll just act like I've been trailing you. You are a suspicious character."

"Yeah, well, you ain't been so straight forward. First you're a gambler who's never set foot on the Mississippi, and then you're a detective, and now you're a marshal. How do I know you ain't Grissom settin' me up?"

"Because you know I'm not."

Will nodded reluctantly. "I reckon."

"Now tomorrow, we'll get the gold in to Walkersville and start some tongues wagging. They'll be watching you like hawks. Then come Saturday night, we'll all go to the dance, and you'll sneak out before it's over. They'll follow, and I'll be up at the mine, waitin'. And the McBrides can stay in town where it's safe."

Will's face darkened as grim thoughts returned. "So we'll finally get Grissom."

"His big mistake was hittin' Pecos Junction. You split 'em up, Tanner. And you killed five of 'em within a short time. I don't think they even knew why you were after 'em, but they hightailed it north."

"Why'd they let the gold sit so long?"

"Nobody dared come after it until Grissom gave the word, and I figure Grissom was planning to get rid of his men and have the gold for himself. You'd already been doing his job for 'im, but I reckon he got scared when you sent Beeker to prison. He must have been real hot under the collar when he found the gold wasn't there."

"Well, we'd better get some sleep if you're settin' me up tomorrow."

In the boys' bedroom, the two men spread their blankets on the wooden floor and rolled into them. They could hear Ricky breathing in his sleep, but Toby was awake, and he leaned over to see Will stretched out near him.

Timidly, Toby reached down and slid his hand into Will's. "You be careful, huh?"

Will squeezed his hand and sniffed. "Yeah, sure."

In the morning, Will headed for town with the bag barely fitting inside his saddlebag. He knew that Harriman was somewhere behind him, and he was glad of it, for waiting for him on the trail was a man he had seen with Fontane the day he had met the McBrides.

He was the one called Switz and was wearing ranch clothes, but his holster was cut down and his hat pushed back. His face was round and hairy, his little eyes set close together.

"You, Tanner."

Will reined up some twenty feet from him and casually leaned forward on the pommel. It was sunny but cool, and the wind was rising.

"Tanner, I got a bone to pick with you."

"That a fact?"

"You killed my friend Packard."

"So?"

"So I'm gonna lay you out right here."

Will felt needles prickling up and down his back. This man was no Trace. It was a setup and likely well paid for, and somewhere in the scattered pines or across the river where the aspens clustered, there was a rifle, aimed for the kill. He wondered where Harriman was.

Will started his horse forward, and Switz straightened in the saddle, confused and not knowing what to do. Will kept riding, and the man dug in his heels, shooting his horse sideways. Will turned his black right after him.

The man kept backing his horse, and Will kept after him.

"Blast you, Tanner, get away from me."

"If I'm gonna be back shot, I want you in the line of fire."

Switz snarled and spun his horse away. As he did, his right hand out of sight, he went for his six-gun, then jerked his horse around and fired.

Will drew and fired so fast, the man couldn't pull the trigger again, and there was a big black mark in the center of his forehead. Switz gasped, mouth wide open, and he dropped the reins and his six-gun. He died sitting up, then toppled like a wooden peg from the saddle, crashing down in the grass.

A rifle cracked, the bullet singing past Will's ear, and he

reined about, dropping low in the saddle as he holstered his six-gun and pulled his Winchester.

He heard one more shot, over in the trees across the river. Straightening, he reached down to calm his horse and listened. There were no more shots. Just Harriman coming from the aspens and fording the river.

"You sure took your time," Will said, shoving his rifle back in the scabbard.

"It was another of Walker's men."

"But it's still not proof."

"We still got our bait. They see that gold, they'll know where it came from, all right. They'll have to show their hand to track you down."

"I hope you're right."

"We'll let Walker come get his own men."

Will rode on ahead, Harriman far behind and keeping mostly out of sight. At length, they reached Walkersville and Will rode into town first, reining up in front of the express office. Pike was sitting on a bench next door, in front of his own office, and glaring at him.

"Mornin', sheriff."

With an easy smile, Will pulled down his saddlebags and strolled into the express office where a clerk with spectacles on the end of his round nose was busy waiting on an elderly miner. Will waited patiently at the counter, his saddlebags over his shoulder. When the miner left, Will was alone with the clerk, and he drew out the sack, shoving it forward.

"I'd like to bank this."

The clerk stared at the name Gila City. "My, my, that's unusual."

"Just weigh it."

"Yeah, sure, but that's a bank sack."

"Is this a bank or what?"

"Well, yeah."

"That miner just deposited his sack with no trouble, so are you going to do your job or what?"

The clerk made a face and looked inside the sack. "But this is pure dust. High grade."

"Just weigh it."

Swallowing, the clerk put it on the scale and kept adding weights until it balanced. "That's a lot of gold, mister."

The clerk wrote out the receipt, and Will shoved it inside his vest pocket. Then he headed back outside into the noonday sun, taking up the reins. Leading his black, he crossed over to the cafe to have himself a meal. At the entrance, he paused to see Harriman riding in, while the clerk was hanging up a closed sign and running over to talk to Pike.

Will went into the cafe and found a table. Through the dirty windows, he saw Pike hurrying across to the gambling hall. Harriman dismounted in front of the express office and took his time loosening the cinch while his sorrel bit at him.

Then Harriman pretended to be looking for Pike and ran into the clerk, who had come running out of the store nearby. Nervous, the clerk skirted the marshal and went back to reopen the express office.

About that time, a gunman came out of the store, got on his horse and headed north out of town, presumably to get Walker.

Harriman reported the deaths of the two men to the express office clerk, who could only stare at him.

"You tell Walker to take care of the bodies." The clerk didn't mention the Gila City gold.

And so it went for three days, a waiting game. It was obvious that Will knew where the gold sacks were, and it was plenty obvious that certain men were going to breathe down his neck if he set one foot out of town.

So he rested. In the cafe. On benches in the sunlight. At the poker table. And in a hotel room. Men were gathering on the boardwalks. All waiting for Will to do something foolish.

TWELVE

And then it was the night of the dance at the McBride town hall. Tables with food lined the walls. The few women in the town were all prettied up, including Eleanor, who sure wasn't wearing black. In fact, her blue silk dress was cut rather low and set down on the shoulders. She had her hair up in thick curls.

Will and Harriman mixed among the ranchers and townsmen. There were a few miners, but they came for the food mostly. Two fiddlers were on a makeshift stage at the back of the hall. Several children ran about using people for cover.

Walker came in a new black coat, his hair slicked back. He headed straight for Eleanor. Then Pike strolled in like a cleaned up grizzly, followed by Domino in his diamond studs and a blue vest. Fontane arrived along with several of the Walker hands.

Then the McBrides came. Maggie looked fetching in a blue-green dress, her graying red hair set back with a jeweled comb, Harriman claiming her right away.

"Maggie, you've stolen my heart."

She blushed and moved into his embrace as the music began. Ricky was using a cane, but he had all of his color back and was joking with local youths. Toby was bantering with some of the youngsters.

And there was Darcie, stunning in a green silk dress with white lace at the throat. Her red hair fell in soft waves on her shoulders, and every young cowhand in the place wanted to dance with her. Will watched her whirl about the floor, and he had a strange feeling of anxiety. Was he jealous?

Then suddenly, she was in front of him. Her freckles danced as she smiled at him, holding out her hand.

The music started, and he paused in front of her. "I don't know how to dance."

"Just walk and skip when I do."

Clumsily, he put his right hand at her waist, her left fingers sliding up his right shoulder. Then he took her other hand in his. Her guidance moved him, but he felt like a fool.

On the other hand, it was worth it to hold her and look down at her pretty face. Her smile gave him pleasure.

The music stopped, and he stood holding her, gazing down at her shining eyes. She was so enticing, he could only stare.

Then a turkey trot started, and they were swept up in it, finishing with laughter. Other men came to dance with her; and Will found himself at the punch table with Harriman.

"You dance like a turkey," Harriman said.

"Yeah, well you look like a dude out there."

The lawman poured himself some punch. "Walker's watching you like a hawk. And so's Domino and every other gun slick. They've got to figure there's more gold where that came from."

"I sure hope you got a fast horse."

"Got two of 'em, remember?"

"Maybe you oughta get going so you'll be in place. They ain't gonna shoot until I find the gold."

"Give me an hour start."

Harriman turned away as Domino came over to Will. He looked slicker than ever, and he smiled as he tweaked his short black beard, his wild eyes gleaming in narrow slits.

"Well, Tanner, I hear you're still pulling the trigger."

"Where are you from, Domino?"

The gambler poured himself some punch, and this time he saw fit to be civil. "Philadelphia."

Will was surprised. "Philadelphia?"

"Some people come from Philadelphia, you know. I was a school teacher. But I got into a little trouble. Oh, nothing you could arrest me for, marshal. A jealous husband."

"So you headed straight for Walkersville."

"No, there was the War Between the States." Domino sipped his punch. "What about you, Tanner? You from Texas?"

"I've been there."

"You killed a lot of men down there."

"They was all wanted."

"I hear you walked in with a sack of gold a few days ago. I got a good place for you to spend it, and our scales are right accurate."

"I'm not a gambler, Domino."

"All men are gamblers, Tanner. You gamble with your life."

With that, Domino smiled, turned, and walked away.

Will waited the full hour, chatting with Timothy and Elmer and Grady, dancing with Maggie and Darcie, and all the while knowing Walker and Pike were watching him carefully. He casually headed for the back door. Then he saw Fontane standing next to it. The big man looked him up and down, then pretended to be watching the dancers.

Will slipped out back to where his black was waiting, along with an obvious packhorse. He drew on his leather coat, tightened the cinch and mounted. Certain he was being watched, he turned and rode behind the buildings of McBride until he got to the bridge. Then he crossed over and headed up an alley in Walkersville, leaving town to head north along the river in the moonlight.

Later that night, the McBrides, disobeying Harriman's orders for them to spend the night in town, headed for home. They had stock to tend and horses to feed and water. And they had no stomach for spending the night in a hotel.

Back at the ranch long after midnight, all they could ' think about was how Will and Harriman could be killed any moment.

With Ricky and Toby in bed asleep, Darcie sat in front of the crackling fire with her mother, both in their dressing gowns and night clothes, both afraid.

"Mom, if anything happens to Will Tanner–"

"Or Marshal Harriman."

"Isn't there anything we can do?"

"No, Darcie."

Darcie was twisting her hands together. "It's not fair. Will was an orphan, raised by a drummer, but when he was fourteen, the drummer died. He was on his own until he married and had a son. Then they were killed."

Maggie looked sad. "When this is all over, I'll tell him the truth."

"What do you mean?"

"I don't want Toby to be hurt."

"Mom, what are you trying to say?"

Maggie stood up and went to her room. She returned with a small box in her hands. "I've kept this hidden all these years."

"What is it?"

Maggie sat down, and opened the box on her lap, the fire blazing up, lighting her face. Darcie came to kneel in front of her.

Maggie drew out a gold locket, letting it dangle from her fingers. "It's Toby's mother."

"But I thought you—"

"No, honey. We adopted Toby when he was a baby."

Darcie stared at her in dismay, then took the locket and carefully snapped it open, gazing at the tiny portrait of a mother and child. "She was beautiful."

"Your father buried her at the Rio Grande. But Toby was alive. He stayed back from the others, kept it from them."

Darcie caught her breath. "Mom—"

"He brought Toby to me, and he became ours. And your father couldn't tell anyone or he'd be tied in with Grissom and could be arrested. And I couldn't tell Will without you and your brothers finding out your father was an outlaw. But now that you already know-"

"Will is Toby's father?"

Maggie nodded. "But don't you see, if Will Tanner dies now, Toby would be losing another father. And this man may die a violent death. And if not, he's still a bounty hunter. How could he take care of a son? And Toby's been mine since I first held him in my arms."

"But Will's got to know before he dies. I'll saddle up."

"You're not going up into those hills. There's going to be

a terrible fight. And I'll not be losing a daughter this night. You're staying here."

"Then I'll give it to him when he comes back."

Reluctant, Maggie let her have the locket. "But if Will Tanner is killed, you are to tell no one. At least not until Toby is older. Don't destroy his childhood with another heartache."

"So Toby really doesn't look like anyone in our family?"

"No, honey. I had to make that up, because he sure does look like Will Tanner. I nearly fell over when Will walked in, and I suspected. But I didn't know for sure until he told me his story about Pecos Junction."

Darcie sat back on the rug, clasping the locket in her slim fingers. She stared at the way it gleamed in the light of the flickering fire as they talked into the night.

Then Maggie went to bed, and it was but two hours to dawn. Darcie stoked up the fire, then hurried into her room and put on her riding clothes. She slipped the locket inside her skirt pocket and pinned it closed, then quietly went back into the front room.

As she pulled down her slicker, she heard a voice.

"Where you goin', Darcie?"

She turned slowly to see Toby rubbing sleep from his eyes as he came out of the boys' room. "You go back to sleep, Toby. I'm just restless."

"Why do you need your slicker?"

"Shh. You'll wake everyone up." She reached for her Winchester.

"Why do you need your rifle?"

"In case Grissom comes this way."

"Then I'd better help you."

"Toby, please, go back to bed."

113

He rubbed his eyes again. "Mom's gonna be mad."

"I'm only going to the barn. Now, please."

Toby mumbled, turned, and went back to his room.

Darcie drew a deep breath and took a box of shells, then slipped outside. It wasn't raining, but it had clouded over. The moon broke through now and then. Her heart was pounding. She didn't want to disobey her mother, but if Will died without knowing his son was alive, it would be a further tragedy.

She knew how to get to the cave and prayed she would not be too late.

Will was riding up through the red rock canyon in the dark, leading his packhorse and hoping Harriman was set up. He knew he was being followed. But he figured he and Harriman could handle Grissom and his two men, whoever they were.

It was drizzling off and on, and he huddled in his leather coat. His black was leaving plenty of tracks in the mud, visible in the occasional moonlight, and he'd soon be at the cavern.

Back along the river a short distance behind Will, seven men reined up to rest their horses, and Pike, in the lead with Fontane, leaned on the pommel of his saddle.

"Well, we'll soon have that gold back."

Fontane grunted. "And take it to Grissom."

"Yeah, but I ain't happy about it."

"You want to cross 'im?"

"No," Pike said. "The Captain's one man I ain't never gonna cross. I like stayin' alive. With my skin attached."

They were sweating despite the predawn chill, because they were both afraid of the man who had ordered them to bring back the gold.

"We'd better get movin' before it rains," Fontane said.

"Yeah, but it's nearly light anyhow, and them prints are set deep in the mud."

The five men they had brought with them included a grimy man with a hairy face, whose curiosity was driving him to push his luck, and he rode up to them.

"Pike, the boys are askin' about the gold."

"You're bein' well paid. And the gold is none of your business."

The man smiled, seemingly satisfied there really was some gold to be found, and he reined about, riding back to the other four gun slicks who were just as curious.

"Why did we bring 'em?" Pike grunted. "Once we get the gold, we won't be able to turn our backs on 'em."

"Grissom's orders. But he didn't say we had to bring 'em back with us. Grissom ain't one to share with strangers."

"And what about with us?"

Fontane wiped his mouth with the back of his hand. "Now that's a worry."

While the men continued after him, Will was riding on up the canyon with his back covered with sweat, knowing they could be on him at any moment. He prayed that Harriman was up there in the trees at the other side of the hollow.

He didn't know that Darcie was on her way from the ranch with frantic news.

Or that Toby was tracking Darcie.

THIRTEEN

First light trickled through the trees as rain fell in the foothills. The dark pines shed it, but the aspens trembled under its weight, and the grass bent as the downpour became heavier.

Riding up the red rock canyon, Will was apprehensive. He had donned his slicker and was bent low in the saddle as water ran furiously off his hat brim. His black was carefully picking its way in the mud. Before long, he would be in the open and be a real target.

Will had planned to take his time, but there was no need, for he caught sight of movement in the rugged terrain that rose high to his left, and he knew Harriman was to be ahead in the trees.

He pulled his slicker more closely about him and over his six-guns, and he rode into the rain, leading the packhorse. As he continued the rest of the way, he was conscious of a rock rolling down the rise to his left.

Knowing he could be dead in seconds, he thought of Darcie's words to him.

"Don't you ever say good-bye to me, Will Tanner."

Miserable in the cold morning rain, he reined up near the cave and dismounted. He stood a moment, then pulled his Winchester from the scabbard. He turned around to scan the rocks as if he was hiding something, and instinct told him they were watching.

He held his Winchester in his left hand. With his right hand, he grabbed some of the thorny brush and jerked and pulled until it revealed the small cave about three feet high.

Up in the rocks, Fontane's mouth was watering.

"We got him hornswoggled."

Pike and Fontane were lying on their bellies on the high rocky terrain, and the men they had with them had scattered.

Down below, Will was on one knee, and he reached in with his right hand, drawing out the sack of dirt they had planted. The cave was slightly uphill, so the sack came easily, and water did not flow inside.

Will drew a deep breath, wondering if he was about to die. "Lord," he whispered, "I hope you're payin' attention."

And a rifle cracked from above. Will spun to see a man hurtling down from the rocks, rolling crazily to the trail. Will's black stayed quiet, but the packhorse was dancing around. Will tossed the sack back into the cave and jumped into the rocks, cocking his rifle.

Up above, Will could see scrambling in the boulders. Harriman was up there in the trees all right, and now they were trying to find out exactly where.

Then a man's hat appeared, and a rifle, and someone was aiming at Will. Firing back, Will hit the hat, and he saw the man roll to the side, arms flailing. Two down.

Another shot from Harriman's way up on the far rise.

Now they knew where he was, and they found cover up in the rocks, while Will waited down below. He knew their horses would be down the canyon, and he wasn't about to let them get there.

He got up and ran back down the canyon, bullets spitting the ground around him, and he dived behind the rocks near where his camp had been.

He could see another gunman, and the man was aiming at him. They both fired at the same time, and the body came rolling over the rocks and disappeared in the brush. Three down.

"Come on," Will muttered, scanning the boulders.

Suddenly, the fourth rose to fire, and Harriman got him in the chest. The man fell backwards and out of sight. Four down.

Up above, the hairy-faced man was sweating in the rain. Working his way back down toward the horses and away from Harriman's fire, the man was suddenly in a position to see Will kneeling in the rocks some twenty feet down from him.

He smiled and nestled in with his rifle, taking careful aim at the crouching Will Tanner.

Before he could pull the trigger, a shot rang out from the trees, hitting him on the side of the head. He screamed, then lurched sideways and fell back into the rocks. Five down.

Harriman had moved clear around to the edge of the rise, and now he showed himself in the rain, waving to Will. A rifle cracked, and Harriman spun around, jerked and fell back into the brush around the trees.

Will knelt quickly, his gaze scanning the rise as his gut churned. The vision of the marshal covered with blood was tearing at him.

"Blast you, Harriman," he murmured.

Moving among the rocks, Will suddenly darted back up the canyon, bullets spitting the mud behind him, He dived into the brush and rolled behind the rocks near the cave.

He could see two men moving quickly on the rise. He fired, missing, but he recognized the big Fontane and the enormous Pike. Both worked for Walker.

"What do you want here, Pike?" Tanner shouted.

"You've got something we want," came the return yell.

"You mean the gold?"

"That's right."

"It's over there in the cave. Come and get it."

"We're in no hurry."

Will began working his way further back into the rocks. He fed more shells into his Winchester, and he checked his Army Colts. He was one man against two now, but they were the meanest. It was not going to be a picnic.

Cold under his wet britches, his leather coat barely protecting the rest of him, water running off his hat, Will was miserable and worried about Harriman.

Up in the rocks, Fontane wiped his wet face. "Harriman's down, but Tanner ain't easy."

"We'll get 'im," Pike said.

"You work your way over there around those rocks and down into the trees. I'll slip back down and get him from the other direction."

Crouched deep in the rocks and brush, Will was sweating under his wet clothes, all the while praying that Harriman was alive. He checked his loads, then moved again, his knees in the mud.

As he came to the edge of the rocks, Will glanced to his right as he saw something in the trees, and he dropped down, afraid to fire in case it was Harriman.

But now Will saw Pike coming around through the trees, which could mean the lawman was dead. Will was grim as he slipped around the rocks, hoping to waylay Pike and take him alive. But the man was so big, he'd take a full load of shot before he could be stopped.

Biting his lip, Will reached the edge of the aspens and knelt behind rocks that were heaped there, grabbing a fallen limb in one hand. Pike came charging around, and Will threw the limb. It caught Pike between the legs, and he went crashing forward, grabbing air as he fell on his belly.

Pike tried to get up, and Will shoved his Winchester right into his neck. "Don't move."

"I ain't movin'."

"Where's Grissom?"

"He ain't here."

"Listen to me, Pike. I can shoot you right now, and nobody'd ever know what happened. I'm a bounty hunter, remember? And you're wanted dead or alive. So where's Grissom?"

"I ain't tellin' you nothin'."

"Well, maybe when they put that noose around your neck, you'll talk."

"Maybe. But I ain't talkin' now."

Will shoved the barrel deep in the man's thick neck and waited a long moment, while Pike's eyes grew round.

And Pike began to whine like a puppy. Will sickened. He drew a deep breath, then reached down and took the man's rifle and six-gun, tossing them aside. "Now take off your belt."

Suddenly, Pike twisted like a sidewinder, hitting Will's legs and knocking him back over the rocks. Will's head struck stone, and he was stunned. In a split second, Pike had pulled a pistol from his boot and was about to shoot Will before he could regain his balance, but a shot rang out, and the bullet hit Pike on the side of his chest.

Pike gasped, half on his knees, the pistol suspended in air then dropping crazily from his fingers. The big man tried to stand, then went back to his knees. He was swaying like a mad man. And then he crumpled up like a rag doll, falling face down.

Will sat up on the rocks, breathing hard.

But Will was terrified, for there was Darcie in the rocks, waving to him. Darcie, some fifty feet from where Fontane had been, huddled in her slicker as she cocked her Winchester again. She had shot Pike, saving Will's life.

Frantic, Will waved her to get down and away, and she dropped out of sight.

Standing with his back to the prone Pike, Will thought the man was dead until he heard a moan. Will spun to see that Pike had somehow survived to grab his pistol and was aiming at Will.

Pike fired, the bullet grazing Will's left shoulder, and Will pulled the trigger on his Winchester, hitting Pike in the throat. Blood spilled forth, and Pike fired again, wildly. Will jumped back and shot him in the heart.

Pike moaned like a giant sea animal, and then he rolled onto his back, lying there in the pouring rain with horror on his face.

Will staggered back, heart pounding. Pike had been one tough hombre. He could feel blood running down his left arm, and he tore off his bandanna, shoving it up inside his coat, but he could feel it was only a crease, a flesh wound. It stung like blazes, though. But he couldn't stop now.

There was still Fontane. And Darcie.

Turning, he started down the canyon at a run. But he stumbled to a halt in the driving rain when he saw Fontane coming up on foot, his left arm around Darcie's neck, his other holding a six-gun to her temple. She had been beaten about the head and blood was being washed down her forehead onto her face. He was half-carrying her, and she looked unconscious.

Fontane was wild-eyed, mouth twisted.

"All right, Tanner. Drop it."

FOURTEEN

Slowly, Will let the Winchester slip down onto the muddy ground, grateful the rain had suddenly stopped. He still had his Colts, but he wouldn't keep them long if he didn't talk fast. And Darcie could be shot at any second as she dangled in Fontane's huge grasp.

"Pike spilled the beans, Fontane. You're Grissom."

"I don't know any Grissom."

"You remember Pecos Junction?"

"What about it?"

"You carried off a woman and child. Left 'em dead at Big Bend. My wife and child."

Fontane stared at him in awe. "So that's it. I wondered what devil was driving you. Well, it was an accident. All this time, you been killin' us off. It was just a dumb accident."

"You got a lot to pay for, Grissom."

"I ain't Grissom. Now drop your gun belt."

"You and your men did a lot of killing in the name of the South and all for greed, makin' a bad mark for all them brave boys who were fightin' for real."

"You listen to me, Tanner. I ain't Grissom. And if you don't drop that gun belt real easy like, I'm going to plug this woman."

"Before you kill me, Fontane, you owe me some answers."

"I don't owe you nothin'. Drop that blasted belt."

"Did you take a potshot at me the first day I got here?"

Fontane grunted. "Nearly missed you."

"Did you kill McBride?"

"Trace done that. The fool wouldn't tell 'im nothin' about the gold."

"And who tried to kill Ricky and Darcie?"

"Trace. He didn't care who he was after, man woman or child. All the same to him."

"Who paid him?"

"Listen here, Tanner—"

"You kill Skip?"

Fontane grinned. "Nah, he caught Walker kissin' his woman. Blew his top and was gonna plug 'em both, and Walker had to kill him."

Will stiffened. "So Walker's Grissom?"

Fontane scowled back at him. "I didn't say that. But it don't matter who Grissom is. I'm gonna plug you clean through anyhow."

"You so scared of Grissom, you can't even tell me who he is before you shoot me down?"

"Everyone's scared of him. He's crazy."

Will shook his head. "And what kind of a man are you, anyhow? You were a top sergeant in the Confederacy. And now you're standing in the mud with a gun held to some innocent girl's head."

"Innocent? She shot Pike easy enough."

124

"Let her go. We'll have it out man to man."

"No deal, Tanner. Drop it."

Darcie was like a rag doll in the big man's grip, and Will worried that she was already dead.

But then something scared him even more.

Moving up behind Fontane was Toby, holding a Winchester as big as he was, aiming it at Fontane's back. Now Toby was shouting.

"Let her go, Fontane, or I'll plug you."

He tried to twist Darcie around, but her boots and skirts were dragging, and he was having trouble with her lifeless body.

He threw her to the ground and spun to fire at Toby, but Will lunged forward and landed on him, knocking him aside. They grappled in the mud, rolling around like greased pigs, fighting to get a grip on each other.

Will slammed his fist in the man's face, and Fontane pounded back. They got to their feet, grappling with each other, Fontane's gun in his hand and Will's iron grip on his fist. They weaved about, gasping for breath.

Fontane's knee came up to hit Will in the gut, and Will slammed his fist in Fontane's belly. They spun around and broke apart, both fighting for breath. Fontane started to fire, but Will lunged and threw the sixgun in the air, sending the shot wild. He pounded Fontane down to his knees and jerked the gun away as he dropped to one knee.

Fontane was breathing hard, trying to rise, and Will hit him hard in the jaw. The man rolled over on his side, barely conscious. Will jerked off the man's belt and used it to tie his hands behind his back good and firm.

Still on one knee and trying to draw breath, Will turned to see Darcie lying on her side with Toby bending over her.

"She's alive," Toby called.

Relieved, Will got to his feet. "Keep your rifle on Fontane. I'm going to find Harriman."

Toby stood up, lifting his Winchester and aiming it at the prone Fontane, who was cussing but unable to move.

Will ran to the trees, searching frantically. He kept losing his footing on the slippery mud.

Where had Harriman fallen?

He stumbled onward, then stopped. There was Harriman lying on his back in the wet grass, his slicker open to show the blood on his shirt, the star glistening on his vest.

Will whispered a prayer and hurried to the lawman. He knelt and laid his hand on the bloody chest. The man's heart was beating.

Will pulled the slicker together to cover Harriman, and he found Harriman's horses far back in the trees. He brought them forward. With a burst of superhuman strength, he got Harriman up on his shoulder, then loaded him across the seat on the bay, tying him down with the lariat from the saddle.

He came through the trees and back down the canyon, leading the bay with the sorrel following, then handed the reins to Toby. He forced the angry Fontane to mount.

Then Will lifted the barely conscious Darcie onto his saddle and mounted behind her, cradling her in his arms. She felt small and cold and lifeless, and she kept trying to talk to him.

"Will, listen to me."

And she would fade out again.

Will would finally have Grissom. Yet it didn't bring back

Jenny or his son. And he could lose Darcie and Harriman. Eight years a dead man, and suddenly, he felt the cold sweat of fear.

Back at the ranch, they discovered that old man Grady was there, his wagon and team near the house. The sun was shining through the moving clouds.

Grady and Ricky lowered Harriman from the saddle and carried him inside. Then Grady returned with his rifle to march Fontane in the house, Toby following. Will swung down and carried Darcie into the warmth, placing her gently in front of the hearth near old Fred, the hound, who was half asleep. He paused a minute to touch Darcie's face.

"Ricky," he said rising, "get me some of that rope by the door. We got to tie Fontane up good."

They hog-tied the big man and left him lying on the floor against the far wall, his hands tied behind his back and to his ankles, his ugly face glaring at them.

Then Toby and Will went down to take care of the horses in the rising wind. The boy was worried, almost frantic.

"What are you going to do now, Will?"

"I'm hoping Fontane will blow the whistle on Grissom."

"Then what? Are you goin' back to Texas?"

"I don't know."

"When will you know?"

Will paused, gazing down at the boy's face in the rain, and he put his hand on Toby's shoulder. "You were pretty brave out there."

Toby grinned with thanks, and they went back up the walk to the house, pausing to see a brilliant rainbow over the foothills. Will prayed it was a good sign.

Inside, they found the unconscious Harriman on the table, bleeding as Maggie worked to get the bullet out with Grady's help.

Darcie was lying barely conscious in front of the fire with Ricky putting towels on her forehead. She moaned some unintelligible words now and then. Then Grady came to help Will off with his coat, and he led him to the fireside to tear off his shirt sleeve, then set about cleaning and bandaging the wound.

Fred watched with disinterest.

Will grunted. "Doesn't that dog care about anything besides eatin' and sleepin'? I bet if you lit a fire under him, he'd just roll over."

Fred lifted his head and lips curled back from his teeth. He growled at Will, and everyone turned to look.

Then Fred howled. Loud and clear.

Will grinned and broke out laughing. Everyone joined in. Fred closed his eyes and went back to sleep, exhausted.

Then Grady finished bandaging Will and made a sling. "Old Fred, he was a great coon hound in his day. But like me, he's gettin' on. That's the first noise I've heard out of him in five years."

Fontane snarled, straining against the ropes. "My friends are gonna get you, Tanner."

Grady rubbed his chin. "Look, Will, I'll get my wagon, and we'll take him in together. You can sleep until we get close to town, and then you can drive, and I'll sit on 'im. And if he moves, I'll blow his head off."

Maggie finished with Harriman, washed her hands and went to kneel with Darcie, who was still conscious off and on. "She may have a concussion. I think we'd better take her and Mr. Harriman in to see Elmer. We'll take our wagon."

"You'd best be far ahead of us," Will said. "What's going on?" Harriman suddenly blurted out, trying to rise. "Where's Tanner?"

Maggie hurried to him, holding him down. "He's all right. Now you lay still."

"Feels like I got shot."

She smiled down at him. "But I got the bullet out. And I sewed you up."

"This keeps up, I'll have to marry you."

Maggie blushed, feeling his brow with her soft hand, fussing over him until he caught hold of her collar with his good hand and pulled her down to him. Their faces were inches apart, but she didn't resist, and he kissed her soundly while everyone stared. When he released her, Maggie's face was pink, and she was blubbering.

Will came over to lean close, telling him about Darcie and Toby, and about the prisoner. The lawman had no color, and he was weak, but he was himself.

"Tanner, I'm still in charge, and don't you forget it. I just lost some blood, that's all. I'll get my strength, back."

Will grinned. "You sure do talk a lot."

"Yeah, but you don't do nothin' without me."

"Want to fight about it?"

"Blast you, Tanner-"

Will turned and started for the door, Maggie following, her eyes wet. "You don't stay alive, you don't get no peach pie."

Will smiled down at her. "Right now, peach pie sounds like the best offer I ever had."

On impulse, he reached down and kissed her on the cheek. She flushed, backing away. He pulled on his leather coat and went to the door.

But Toby was at his side, tugging at his sleeve.

"Will, can I ride with you and Grady?"

"You got to help your sister."

Ricky came over. "Look, I'm goin' with you."

Will shook his head. "No, you've got to take care of the wounded. You've shown you're a full grown man, and that's what's got to be drivin' your wagon, because we don't know what's ahead of us. No tellin' if you're all out of the woods."

Ricky swelled up at the compliment. "Okay."

"But you drive ahead of us and get over to McBride before me and Grady come drivin' in with Fontane."

Both wagons were loaded in the noonday sun with Harriman constantly muttering as he was forced into the McBride's. The clouds had drifted to the south, and the sky was eggshell blue. There was no wind, but it was damp and cold.

Will lifted Darcie in his arms, ignoring his still painful wounds. Her head rolled against his shoulder, and he looked down at her freckled face and long lashes. Her head was heavily bandaged, but soft waves of red hair spread on her shoulders.

He prayed she would wake up and smile again, and he set her in the McBride wagon with the grumbling, protesting Harriman. Maggie climbed in the back to cradle the lawman, who settled down to enjoy her comfort, and Toby held Darcie across his lap. Will covered them all with blankets, and Ricky took up the reins.

Following the McBride wagon at a far distance, Grady drove while Will slept in the wagon bed near Fontane, who was again hog-tied and swearing. Fred, disgusted with the noisy prisoner, crawled over to hide behind Will.

It was late afternoon when Grady reined up along the river. "Will, come on, wake up."

Will jerked awake and sat up. He rubbed his eyes and stumbled to his feet, then climbed up on the wagon seat.

"Okay, but you get down low, Mr. Grady. You're the only one knows how to grow them peaches."

Will took the reins and held the team as Grady crawled into the back with his rifle. Will straightened, gazing far ahead along the river, and he could see the McBride wagon moving toward the distant buildings of Walkersville.

Grady smiled as he moved up behind the wagon seat and away from the snarling Fontane.

"Tell me somethin', Will," Grady said. "When you was carrying Darcie to the wagon, I saw somethin' real interestin' in your face. You gonna settle down here?"

"Not likely."

"Maggie told me about your wife and son. But you can't go through life bein' scared of gettin' hurt again. This is rough country out here. It can happen to any of us. They all like you fine, and Toby thinks you can walk on water. And you and me, we could go fishin' now and then. I know where there's the granddaddy of all trout."

Will shook his head. "Havin' Toby around would be too hard on me. A constant reminder. As it was, I near went crazy when I first saw him. He looks just like my son would have. Except my boy had blue eyes."

"How old was your son when you lost him?"

"Six weeks."

"I hate to tell you this, Will, but babies most always have blue eyes when they're born. But they are just as likely to grow up with some other color, like brown. Maybe you ain't been around babies much."

"You mean Toby could have had blue eyes as a child?"

"That's right."

Will drew a deep painful breath, but he knew wishful thinking wasn't enough. He remembered the wooden cross down by the Rio Grande. *Woman and child, Pecos Junction.*

Ahead in McBride, Walker was waiting in front of the hotel to have supper with Eleanor. She was coming across the street, looking gorgeous in her red outfit. Timothy came out of the hotel as she came to take Walker's hand.

But Sedge was looking past her, toward the bridge, seeing the McBride wagon coming across, the horses dark with sweat. He frowned, walking around her for a better look.

"Sedge, is something wrong?"

"That's Ricky McBride driving the wagon. And his family lying down in the back. Looks like trouble."

The wagon pulled up, and Ricky glanced at Walker with a scowl, then jumped down. "Timothy, can you get Elmer? The marshal's hurt real bad. So's Darcie."

Timothy turned and darted into the hotel, while Walker pretended to be concerned. "I'll help carry them inside."

But Elmer and Timothy came out with two other men, and they carried the marshal inside. Ricky lifted his sister in his arms, and Toby was glaring at Walker as he helped his mother out of the wagon.

"What happened?" Walker asked.

No one answered, and they all went inside the hotel.

Eleanor turned to Walker. "What's it all about, Sedge?"

"All I know is, Tanner deposited some pure gold dust at the express office. Maybe some of the men in town followed him to find out if there was more. They must have run into Harriman. But I don't know what happened to Tanner."

"You mean the McBride gold? But that was to be ours."

"Don't worry, honey, if they found it, we'll get our hands on it, one way or another."

"That's what I like about you, Sedge. Nothing stops you."

He squeezed her hand, then stiffened, for he could see another wagon rolling into Walkersville.

"I think that's Grady," Walker said. "I'm going over to have a look. You go on home."

Walker didn't look back as he hurried across the bridge past the first saloon. When he was near the gambling hall, he saw Grady driving up to the sheriff's office.

And then Tanner and Fontane rose from the wagon bed.

Color drained from Walker's face. Fontane would tell all if his neck was in a noose. Domino must have sent them out after Tanner. Now Walker was the one who would have to suffer if Fontane started talking too much.

Walker was sweating, and he turned to look across the street where Domino was standing in the entrance of his gambling hall, looking as arrogant and unperturbed as ever.

Walker looked back to the wagon.

There was no sign of the gold.

Grady's rifle was across his knees, aimed at Walker.

"They're all dead," Grady said. "Pike and five of your men."

"What were they doing out there?"

"Huntin' gold. And tryin' to ambush a U.S. Marshal and

Mr. Tanner here."

"I didn't know anything about it."

But Walker jumped as Tanner jerked Fontane to a sitting position.

FIFTEEN

W̲alker turned and hurried over to the gambling hall. Will had freed Fontane's legs and was shoving him out of the wagon and into the jail. Grady, rifle in hand, remained on the wagon seat. When he was certain Will was inside, the old man climbed down and backed into the doorway, keeping his eye on the street. Fred stayed in the wagon, his nose over the side.

Will cut Fontane's bonds and shoved him into a cell, locking the door. Exhausted and with his left shoulder still hurting, mostly from the tight bandage, he sat down at the desk.

It was a simple jail with one cell in the back and small, boarded windows on the sides and front. The desk was to the right of the entrance, and the cot was over on the left. A small iron stove was set in the corner behind the desk. Will slumped wearily.

"I'll get Elmer to look at your shoulder," Grady said.

"No, it was just a crease. You can clean it up if it needs it."

Grady leaned out the door and peered into the twilight. "Here comes Ricky, driving his wagon."

"I told them to stay in McBride."

But Ricky jumped down from the wagon and came hurrying inside, his freckled face flushed. Grady shoved the door closed as Will turned up the lamp on the desk.

"Harriman's cussin' up a storm," Ricky said.

"And Darcie?" Will asked.

"Elmer says it's trauma and a bad concussion, but she'll be all right. Whenever she opens her eyes, she asks for you, but she ain't really conscious."

"What shape is Harriman in?"

"He's out there in the wagon, waitin' for us to bring him inside. Maggie and Elmer were fit to be tied, but the marshal insisted."

Will turned the lamp out, and the three men went outside. Grady held the rifle and watched up and down the darkening street. Ricky and Will lifted the muttering, heavily bandaged lawman by his arms and legs and carried him inside, then set him on the cot. Harriman would not lie down and sat against the wall for support.

Under protest, Ricky then drove the wagon back across .the bridge. Grady took his wagon and Fred out to the McBrides' and his own place to tend their stock.

Will barred the door, then went to the desk to tum up the lamp. He was alone with Harriman and the prisoner. He set about building a fire and making coffee while the lawman moaned and cussed where he slumped against the wall.

Will grinned. "I'm going to wash your mouth out with soap."

"You ain't man enough."

"Look at you, all bandaged up and your gun arm in a sling. You ain't gonna be no help."

"Listen to me, Tanner, on my worst day, I can whup the likes of you."

Fontane was banging on the bars. "Let me out of here. I'll make a deal."

Harriman turned painfully to look at him. "Yeah?"

"Let me sneak out of town tonight, and I'll give you Walker."

"How's that?"

"He paid Trace to make McBride tell where the gold was, but Trace killed 'im accidental. And when Maggie wouldn't say yes, Walker figured the kids was stoppin' her, so he sent Trace to get 'em. He was bound to get that gold."

"Your word against Walker's. And Trace is dead."

"Walker's been skimmin' off the express shipments. And stealin' from the mail."

Harriman nodded. "I already know that."

Fontane grew anxious. "And he's a wanted man."

Will slowly walked over to stand near the prisoner, and he could feel his heart going crazy. "He's Grissom?"

"You keep askin' about Grissom. I don't know no Grissom."

Will frowned. "Then who's Walker?"

Harriman answered. "Sedge Wakefield. He's an embezzler. Never was a real lawyer. Just a confidence man. Been a reward out on him for a long time."

Will turned, annoyed. "You went right along with me sayin' he was Grissom."

Harriman grinned. "I can't tell you everything, now can I?"

Realizing there was no deal, the prisoner was furious, near bending the bars with his big hands, shaking them and kicking at them, then yelping when he hurt his foot.

Fontane staggered back to sit down on the cot and growl to

himself. He was so big he filled half the cell. There wouldn't be much room for Walker.

"So who's Grissom?" Will asked the lawman as he sat down at the desk, exhausted from Harriman's double talk.

"I don't know for sure."

"Why don't I believe you?"

Harriman grinned and stretched out on the cot.

Later that night, with Fontane snoring, Harriman was feeling better and sitting up while Will brought him coffee and beans.

Will pulled up a chair, coffee cup in hand. "I thought for sure Fontane and Pike and Trace come up here with Grissom."

"Yeah, they did."

"But Fontane just said—"

"Fontane's too scared of Grissom to talk, unless he's facin' a rope, and we don't have enough to hang 'im."

"But Grissom must have given 'em the orders to follow me," Will said, balling his hands into fists.

"Maybe so, whoever Grissom is. But as soon as I'm up to it, we'll be arrestin' Walker for murder and conspiracy. Along with the old charge of embezzlement."

"And putting him in the same cell as Fontane?"

"Sure will be interesting. But Fontane's not afraid of Walker. Fontane's not afraid of anybody but Grissom."

Will was disgruntled all night.

And so was Walker, who went to see Domino in the morning, having coffee with him in the gambling hall. They sat at a table, and Walker wiped his brow. The gambler's eyes were near white as he snickered.

"Walker, you're sure a nervous coyote this morning."

"Listen, Domino, don't play games with me. Pike and the

rest are all dead, and Fontane's in there shooting off his mouth to save his own skin. And I figure you sent those boys out after Tanner. So you have an obligation here."

Domino snickered. "Look, Walker, I let you be the big he-bull around here because it suited me. Don't push your luck."

"Fontane could probably tell a few things about you."

"He wouldn't have the guts," Domino said. "Now you want to get rid of Fontane? Why don't you get Prudo to take care of Tanner? That'd make it easier to get to Fontane. The marshal's hurt bad, and he's got no help."

"Prudo won't be fast enough."

"He might get lucky."

While Domino and Walker talked in the gambling hall, Elmer came to the jail to look at Harriman and reported that Darcie was sleeping and would be all right.

"Harriman, you're made of hard rock iron," Elmer said, shaking his head. "And that Maggie sure should have been a doctor. This isn't the first time I've seen what she can do with a knife!"

"She'd make a fine wife," the lawman said. "And this would be a good place for a man like me to retire."

"She'd not have the likes of you," Elmer snapped. "Me and Timothy, we been courtin' her a lot longer."

Harriman grinned. "You can dance at our weddin'."

While the two men bantered back and forth, Will became uneasy and went out the door, wanting to see the sunlight and the glow in Darcie's red hair, but wondering if a man like him could ever rest easy.

Outside, Will paused in front of the jail. Prudo was coming out of the hall, moving past Walker and swaggering onto the boardwalk, his hat pushed back from his curly brown hair, his smooth face twisted in an oily smile.

"Tanner."

Will paused, his mouth dry. He had killed enough men, and he was in no hurry to shoot down another gunman with an itchy finger.

"Back off, Prudo."

"You and me, we got some unfinished business."

"I got no time for you."

Men appeared in doorways. An incoming rider reined up and halted out of the line of fire. Walker was still behind the swinging doors, watching.

"I'm going to kill you, Tanner. Whether you draw or not, so you'd better be paying attention."

Will started walking toward him. "I'm going to flatten your nose so it sticks out your ears."

Prudo stiffened, hand near his gun. "Stop right there, Tanner."

But Will kept walking toward him, and Prudo began to back away, mouth twisted in anger. Will was within eight feet when Prudo's fingers started to rise toward his six-gun.

Will dived forward, slamming his fist in the man's gut, and Prudo gasped, eyes round, staggering back. Will grabbed his hat and slapped him across the face with it. He hit him again in the belly, and when Prudo's head came down, he brought it up with a blow from his fist.

Prudo snapped back, trying to talk, out of breath, face white, hands trying frantically to grab at Will.

Will hit him again, and Prudo dropped to his knees.

"Now you listen to me," Will said. "I've just saved your life.

And if I were you, I'd get out of town and start over somewhere else."

Prudo couldn't talk, and he was doubled up.

Will turned and started walking away, but he heard that click of a hammer. He spun, drew, and fired, hitting Prudo square in the chest before the man could pull the trigger. Prudo came forward, wretching, and dropped to the ground on his belly, arms flailing.

And then he was dead. Will stood with his Colt in hand, his stomach churning. There had been no need for this man to die, except for someone's bidding.

Walker came out of the Golden Wheel and called to him. "Tanner."

Will paused as the well-dressed embezzler came across the street to pause near him in front of the jail. "Here's another one of your men you can bury, Walker."

"Mr. Walker to you, Tanner. How's Fontane?"

"Sweating."

Walker straightened his small-brimmed hat. "So you and the marshal are taking him somewhere for trial?"

"No judge here."

"But you really came here looking for Grissom, isn't that right?"

Will stiffened, looking him over. "And you know who Grissom is?"

"Yes, I do. But you'll have to release Fontane."

"Well, then, let's talk to the marshal."

Will turned, still not trusting the man, and opened the door to let Walker stroll past in front of him. Inside, Harriman, sitting at the desk, broke into a smile.

"Well, Mr. Walker, visiting so early in the day?"

Fontane sat up in his cell, hope bright in his face.

"I came to see about letting this man out of jail."

"You have something to trade?"

"Grissom."

Fontane jumped to his feet, wild-eyed, grabbing the bars. "No, don't tell 'em. He'll think I done it. You can't tell 'em, Walker. If you do, I'll be a dead man."

Harriman leaned back in his chair, studying Walker. "So you want to trade Fontane for Grissom."

"That's right."

"Well, you're too late," Harriman said. "Fontane's already given us you, Mr. Wakefield."

Walker's eyes bugged. "What?"

"You're an embezzler."

Swallowing hard, Walker tried to get his mouth going. "You're making a mistake. All I want to do is get Fontane out. Then I'll give you Grissom."

"He's also tagged you for murder and conspiracy."

"You have no evidence but the word of a man who's trying to save his own skin," Walker snapped, sweat on his handsome face. "And I never heard of anyone named Wakefield. If you want to do business, I'll be at the Golden Wheel."

Walker turned on his heel with his back to them as he started to leave. His right hand slid under his coat, grasping his six-gun.

"Hold it, Walker," said Harriman. "You're under arrest."

Walker stopped, pulled his weapon and drew back the hammer, then spun around.

Only to have Will's big fist slam into his face, smashing his nose and front teeth. Walker yelped, dropped his revolver and grabbed his face and bleeding nose.

"You broke my nose! You broke my tooth!"

Despite himself, Will was smiling over clenched teeth, and he grabbed Walker by the arm, marching him over to the cell. Fontane was grinning and chuckling as Walker was shoved into the cell, the door locked behind him.

"You ain't so pretty now," Fontane said to Walker.

Holding his nose, blood dripping through his fingers, Walker sounded strange as he searched for his hand-kerchief. "No, wait. We can make a deal."

Harriman shook his head. "I want Grissom pretty bad, but you're a wanted man, Walker. And our deal's going to be with Fontane. He'll be testifying against you."

"Yeah," Fontane said.

Walker was anxious, near frantic. "When I hired Fontane, he let slip who Grissom was. And he told me about Grissom's gold. You let me out, I'll give him to you."

"He's lying," Fontane said, quickly.

"You can't take this man's word," Walker said. "He's afraid. Now get me some water."

Fontane grabbed the bars. "For Pete's sake, Walker, don't tell 'em. We'll both be skinned alive. I seen him do it twice in the Nations. And that's one horrible way to go. You think he's got crazy eyes, you oughta see him really go crazy."

Will stared at the frightened, blubbering Fontane. Who was this Grissom that could turn a huge man's knees to water?

Will turned to Harriman. "I'm going after Domino."

"You don't know he's Grissom."

"He's the only one with crazy eyes."

Walker looked up. "He's Grissom, all right. But you got no chance, Tanner. The man's insane."

SIXTEEN

W ill checked the load in both his six-guns and charged out of the jail, nearly stumbling into Eleanor, who was wearing a pretty yellow outfit and who smiled at him, flirting.

"Why, Mr. Tanner, you're truly in a hurry."

"Yes, Ma'am."

"Have you seen Mr. Walker this morning?"

"He's in jail."

She was startled. "What?"

"You want his ranch, you'd better marry him afore he gets shipped off to stand trial."

"Why is he in jail?"

"The marshal will set you straight."

Will turned his back on her and was about to cross the street when he paused. Domino was standing in front of his gambling hall, right next to his fully packed horse. The man's pale eyes were glowing like lamplights under his heavy brows as he rested his hand on the saddle.

Will moved off the boardwalk, his mouth tight. He had waited eight years for this.

Domino moved into the sunlight, pushing his coat back from his six-gun, but smiling. "Well, Mr. Tanner, you look like a man with bad news."

"Fontane just spilled his guts, Grissom. And Walker's backing him up."

"I don't know what you're talking about."

"You, Trace and Pike and Fontane. Come up here to get the gold you'd stashed, but McBride had hidden it. So you made yourselves at home and played a waiting game."

Domino sneered. "They sure have been giving you a lot of hogwash."

Will could hardly breathe. He was aware of Harriman in the doorway of the jail, and he moved farther into the street, keeping the lawman out of the line of fire. He kept talking as Domino snickered.

"When McBride starting spending some of the gold, you figured he knew where it was for sure. But Walker beat you to it, and McBride ended up dead. But you saw how Walker was going after Maggie, so you just sat back and waited for him to find it for you."

"You tell a good story, Tanner."

"You must have busted a gut when I brought in that Gila City bag of gold. And it was you sent Pike and Fontane and the others after me, knowing they was so scared of you, they'd bring it back. That's how you worked it, Grissom. Skinning your deserters alive to keep the others in line."

"You have no proof."

"You took my wife and child from Pecos Junction. You were responsible for their deaths."

Domino was stunned. "That's why you've been dogging our

trail? All these years? The whole thing was an accident."

"If you hadn't grabbed her, they'd both be alive now."

Domino was suddenly grim, realizing he had just put his foot in his mouth. He had always been so much smarter than anyone else, and now he was reddening, mouth working. Will wasn't going to let up.

"So you're admitting your name is Grissom."

"I'm not admitting one thing, Tanner."

"You were an officer for the Confederacy. How did you turn into an animal?"

"I think you're trying to get me to draw on you."

Will was grim, sweat trickling down his back. "Well?"

"You have no proof of anything. Just the babbling of a couple of fools."

"They'll swear to it in court."

Domino slowly pushed his hat back from his damp brow. "I can tell you what's going to happen here. I'm going to kill you, and then I'm riding out."

"I waited eight years for this. You're not going any place but jail. Taking my wife and child was a felony, and they died from it. That's murder. And you're going to hang."

"I'm leaving, and you can't stop me, Tanner. No man has ever beaten me to the draw."

They stood facing each other in the street, the sun warm above them, casting their shadows downward. At any moment, one or both of them could be dead.

Will's hands rested at his sides. He felt an intense pressure to end this and a terrible fear that Grissom was faster.

There was a hush in the street. Harriman was in the doorway some distance from and behind Will. Domino was standing in the street like death itself.

Sweat trickled down Will's back and rear.

Suddenly, Domino hunched a little, and the, man drew, but Will drew at the same time, their six-guns leaping into their hands and firing simultaneously.

Domino's shot hit Will above the right shoulder, cutting the flesh and knocking him back a step. Shock ran down Will's right arm, and he caught his breath as he tried to hold on to his six-gun.

Will's first shot hit Domino in the chest. The man dropped to his knees, firing into the dirt, his crazy eyes so wild there was no color at all, just blank spots under his brows. He raised his weapon and aimed at Will, pulling the trigger as Will fired again. Domino's shot went wild, but Will's thudded into his chest.

Domino was still on his knees, staring unseeingly.

Will walked slowly forward, and he paused a few feet away. "Why, Grissom? What made you this way?"

Eyes white and glazed, Domino was shuddering. Then he slowly collapsed, face down in the street.

Will was aware of the blood dribbling down his arm, but he knew he wasn't hurt bad. He felt no pain, because nothing could hurt him now.

It was over. He felt stone cold, drained.

But Harriman was suddenly at his side. "Get back in the jail and let Elmer tend to you. And then I'll send him to tell Maggie and the others we'll be along come evenin', as soon as I deputize a couple men to watch the jail."

It was twilight when Will, his right arm in a sling, strolled down the street toward McBride with Harriman, whose left arm was in a sling as well.

They paused as Eleanor and the little preacher came up the street. "More shooting?" she asked, annoyed.

"Don't worry," Harriman said. "Walker's all right."

"We'll be married tonight so I can help him," she said. "He's going to need me to run things for him."

The preacher smiled with his eyes misting. "Love is a wonderful thing."

Harriman and Will stood aside as she hurried toward the jail with the preacher on her heels, and they watched them go inside.

"Interesting," Harriman said.

"She's sure after his holdings."

"Well, the trouble is, we'll be confiscatin' most everything he's got, on account of his embezzlement and the way he was skimming from the mail and the gold shipments. I doubt there'll be anything left."

"You're not going to tell her?"

Harriman grinned, and Will had to grin back.

But as they started walking again, they both sobered, and Harriman looked at Will, who was drained and colorless.

"You all right, Tanner?"

"I'm just glad it's done with."

"Well, you rushed things a little. Domino matched Grissom's description clear enough, but I was waiting on my witnesses to arrive."

Will stopped short, suddenly angry. "You had a description of Grissom?"

"Sure, from his former commanding officer in the Confederacy, a colonel who hated Grissom's guts."

"All this time you knew it was Domino?"

Harriman grinned. "Well, sure."

"You let me think it was Walker."

"You said it, not me."

"Blast you, Harriman. Why didn't you tell me?"

"I didn't want you killed."

"What?"

"You sort of growed on me. Like tree moss."

They crossed the bridge, and Will was shaking his head, glaring at the grinning lawman. Then he was resigned to the fact that Harriman was always going to be this way. Never a dull moment. But he sure liked the man.

They walked up to the hotel, finding Darcie alone on the outside steps, wearing a heavy shawl and a blue dress, her red hair spilling down her shoulders. She was pale but lovely, and Will felt his mouth go dry.

Harriman went on into the hotel, and Will removed his hat with his left hand. He felt dirty and rumpled, but he sure was glad to see her.

"You saved my life," he said.

"Toby saved us both."

"But you look all right."

"So do you." She moved a step closer, her smile fetching and sweet. "And I've finally figured out your name. It's Willoughby."

Even in the fading light, Will's face turned red as a beet. "You tell anyone, I'll whup you."

She put her hand on his arm, her touch radiating his neck down to his boots. She sure was pretty, and her smile was enough to turn a man to jelly, which was happening real fast about now.

She slid her hands up his shirt to his neck, pulling his head down. He didn't resist. She was kissing him, her sweet lips like honey, her warmth pressed against him.

He fell apart and began kissing her back, crushing her to him with his left arm, his head spinning. He couldn't stop kissing her, but at length she drew back in the fold of his arm.

Her eyes were luminous in the night. "You can't leave us, Will. It would break my mother's heart if you took him away."

"What are you talking about?"

"Toby. He's your son."

Will fell away from her, his knees turning to water, gut churning. "Toby?"

"He's your son. Mom told me how our father had found the baby alive by the river, and he brought him home. They were afraid to tell anyone because it might tie him into Grissom, and he'd be arrested."

Will leaned sideways, then backward, barely able to stand. It was too much to grasp, to accept, to believe.

She drew the locket from her pocket, handing it to him. It was icy cold in his hot fingers, and it glittered in the moonlight. His brain was pounding until he wanted to scream,

"Father took this from your wife before he buried her."

Painfully, he opened the clasp, staring at the portrait of his wife and child. "My God. Toby's my son?"

"Mom was afraid to tell you because she thought you were going to be killed. And I think she was afraid you wouldn't stop being a bounty hunter. But now, she knows it's the right thing to do. You've turned into a hero."

"My son," he whispered, eyes brimming.

They heard running steps from inside the hotel, and Toby came scurrying out with a grin, Maggie and Harriman on his

151

heels, followed by Ricky. Will gazed at Toby as he choked back his emotions. The boy was excited, coming right up to him with a big grin.

"Hey, Will, the marshal said you was here. I'm sure glad you're okay. Boy, just like in them novels, huh."

"My God, you are my son."

Toby caught his breath, staring from him to Darcie. Harriman held a tearful Maggie to his side as Ricky took his mother's arm. The boy was dazed, eyes wide and mouth open.

Darcie smiled and took his hand. "It's true, Toby. You're really only eight and a half. Father saved you when your mother died. And there's the locket she wore."

Toby looked so small as Will surrendered the locket to him, that Will's heart was about to break. Toby held it open in the light from the hotel, his hands shaking. He closed the locket and clasped it tight in one hand. He gazed up at Will with wonder.

"You're really my Pa?"

Will dropped to one knee as tears filled his eyes, and he gazed longingly at the boy, aching to grab him, yet terrified of rejection.

"Is it all right with you, son?"

Toby's face lit up with a joyous smile. "Sure is."

The boy fell into Will's arms. They both cried and hugged and kissed as Darcie wept. Then Will lifted him up like his child and held him.

"Gee whiz," Toby said, wiping his tears. "Now I got two moms and two fathers. And when Mom and the marshal get married, I'll have three fathers. And if you marry Darcie, I'll have three moms. I'm a lucky kid."

"I reckon so," Will murmured, afraid to look at Darcie.

"And we'll all go fishin' with Grady and Fred."

"Sounds mighty fine."

Darcie put her chin in the air. "Will Tanner, you're going to have to do better than that." She turned and started walking down the boardwalk in the moonlight.

Toby was sniffing and grinning as Will set him down.

"Go get her, Pa."

Will squeezed the boy's shoulder and hurried along behind Darcie. "Will you wait up?"

"Do you love me?"

"I love your biscuits."

She spun around and put her hands on her hips, glaring at him in the pale light. "And?"

He was fumbling all over himself. "Your freckles. Are you gonna marry me or not?"

She giggled and fell into his arms to nestle against him as he kissed her honey lips. Then he reached for Toby and pulled him into their embrace.

Never again would Will be the young, innocent man he had been at twenty, nor the deadly hunter who had tracked the men down for eight years, for both had died in the street with Grissom.

He was new and alive and reborn.

He was Willoughby Tanner, starting over.

But anyone who called him that had better smile.

ABOUT THE AUTHOR

Western novelist and screenwriter **Lee Martin** grew up on cattle ranches in Northern California. Martin began writing in the third grade and, later in life, wrote and sold 43 short stories before turning to novels with 23 now published. Martin is also a prolific writer of screenplays, mostly Westerns.

Martin's recent novels, *The Grant Conspiracy*, *The Last Wild Ride*, and *Fury at Cross Creek*, all received rave reviews from *True West Magazine* and were based on Martin's screenplays, as is *Fast Ride to Boot Hill*. *In Mysterious Ways*, Martin's new modern suspense Western, received great critical acclaim from *Kirkus Reviews* and *Midwest Book Reviews*. *Trail of the Fast Gun* is the first book of seven in The Darringer Brothers series, all of which have been reissued in paperback and ebook by Vaca Mountain Press, along with many of Martin's earlier novels.

Martin left the practice of law to write full-time, primarily concentrating on Western screenplays and novels, and often converting one to the other. Martin's screenplay for *Shadow on the Mesa*, starring Kevin Sorbo, Wes Brown, and Gail O'Grady, was based on Martin's novel of the same title (Five

Star Publishing, 2014). The movie was the second-highest-rated and second-most-watched original movie in Hallmark Movie Channel's history when it premiered in 2013. The film also won the prestigious Wrangler Award given by the National Cowboy & Heritage Museum in Oklahoma City for Best Original TV Western Movie. Several of Martin's screenplays are currently under option by producers. *The Siege at Rhyker's Station* and *The Desperate Riders*, based on two of Martin's screenplays, are both being filmed in the Fall of 2020, and will eventually be available as novels. To learn more, visit Lee Martin Westerns on Facebook.

www.ingramcontent.com/pod-product-compliance
Lightning Source LLC
Chambersburg PA
CBHW031238260626
47169CB00007B/2355

LEE MARTIN
TRACK THE MEN DOWN

It's the spring of 1876, and for the last eight years, Will Tanner has been tracking down the Grissom Gang in order to avenge the murder of his wife and son. Will has left six dead men in his wake and another in prison, but still, he cannot rest… because Grissom himself—along with four of his men—is still alive.

Will suspects the gang's gone north to Colorado Territory, and his search takes him through the town of McBride where he meets a spunky widow named Darcie. He's tipped off there that the gang may be holed up in Walkersville—a notorious hangout for killers. As a known bounty hunter, Will quickly becomes the target of every wanted man in the valley. With the help of Darcie and her family, he continues his relentless and dangerous pursuit of every last member of the gang. But when Will discovers that all along the gang's been after Confederate gold, he knows there's one chance in a thousand that he'll come out of this alive…

Look for… The Darringer Brothers Series, *Black River,* *The Maverick Gun, Dead Man's Trail, The Lone Rider,* *Valley of the Lawless,* and **MORE** by Lee Martin!

Available in ebook and paperback from Vaca Mountain Press on Amazon.com

VACA MOUNTAIN PRESS

Facebook: Lee Martin Westerns

Western / Action / Adventure $17.99

ISBN-13: 978-1-952380-41-9

51799

9 781952 380419